Goosebumps

COLLECTION 13

Goosebumps

COLLECTION 13

Night of the Living Dummy III
Bad Hare Day
Egg Monsters From Mars

R.L. Stine

Scholastic Children's Books,
Commonwealth House, 1–19 New Oxford Street, London WC1A 1NU, UK
a division of Scholastic Ltd
London ~ New York ~ Toronto ~ Sydney ~ Auckland
Mexico City ~ New Delhi ~ Hong Kong

First published in this edition by Scholastic Ltd, 1999

Night of the Living Dummy III
Bad Hare Day
Egg Monsters From Mars
First published in the US by Scholastic Inc., 1996
First published in the UK by Scholastic Ltd, 1997

ISBN 0 590 63774 6
All rights reserved

Typeset by Rowland Phototypesetting Ltd, Bury St Edmunds, Suffolk
Printed by Cox & Wyman Ltd, Reading, Berks.

10 9 8 7 6 5 4 3 2 1

CONTENTS

Goosebumps

Night of the
Living Dummy III

The stairs up to my attic are narrow and steep. The fifth step is loose and wobbles when you stand on it. All the other stairs creak and groan.

My whole house creaks and groans. It's a big, old house. And it's kind of falling apart. Mum and Dad don't really have the money to repair it.

"Trina—hurry!" my brother, Dan, whispered. His words echoed in the steep attic stairwell. Dan is ten, and he is always in a hurry.

He's short and very skinny. I think he looks like a mouse. He has short brown hair, dark eyes, and a pointy little chin. And he's always scurrying around like a mouse searching for a place to hide.

Sometimes I call him Mouse. You know. Like a nickname. Dan hates it. So I only call him Mouse when I want to make him mad.

Dan and I don't look at all like brother and sister. I'm tall and I have curly red hair and

3

green eyes. I'm a little chubby, but Mum says not to worry about it. I'll probably slim down by the time I'm thirteen, next August.

Anyway, no one would ever call me Mouse! For one thing, I'm a lot braver than Dan.

You have to be brave to go up to our attic. Not because of the creaking stairs. Or the way the wind whistles through the attic windows and makes the panes rattle. Not because of the dim light up there. Or the shadows. Or the low ceiling covered with cracks.

You have to be brave because of the eyes.

The dozens of eyes that stare at you through the darkness.

The eyes that never blink. The eyes that stare with such eerie, heavy silence.

Dan reached the attic ahead of me. I heard him take a few steps over the squeaking, wooden floorboards. Then I heard him stop.

I knew why he'd stopped. He was staring back at the eyes, at the grinning faces.

I crept up behind him, moving on tiptoe. I leaned my face close to his ear. And I shouted, "BOO!"

He didn't jump.

"Trina, you're about as funny as a wet sponge," he said. He shoved me away.

"I think wet sponges are funny," I replied. I admit it. I like to annoy him.

"Give me a break," Dan muttered.

4

I grabbed his arm. "Okay." I pretended to break it in two.

I know it's stupid. But that's the way my brother and I kid around all the time.

Dad says we didn't get our sense of humour from him. But I think we probably did.

Dad owns a little camera shop now. But before that he was a ventriloquist. You know. He did a comedy act with a dummy.

Danny O'Dell and Wilbur.

That was the name of the act. Wilbur was the dummy, in case you didn't guess it.

Danny O'Dell is my dad. My brother is Dan, Jr. But he hates the word junior, so no one ever calls him that.

Except me. When I want to make him *really* mad!

"Someone's left the attic light on," Dan said, pointing to the ceiling light. The only light in the whole attic.

Our attic is one big room. There are windows at both ends. But they are both caked with dust, so not much light gets through.

Dan and I made our way across the room. The dummies all stared at us, their eyes big and blank. Most of them had wide grins on their wooden faces. Some of their mouths hung open. Some of their heads tilted down so we couldn't see their faces.

Wilbur—Dad's first dummy, the original

Wilbur—was perched on an old armchair. His hands were draped over the chair arms. His head tilted against the chair back.

Dan laughed. "Wilbur looks just like Dad taking a nap!"

I laughed, too. With his short brown hair, his black glasses, and his cheesy grin, Wilbur looked *a lot* like Dad!

The old dummy's black-and-yellow checked sports jacket was worn and frayed. But Wilbur's face was freshly painted. His black leather shoes were shiny.

One wooden hand had part of the thumb chipped out. But Wilbur looked great for such an old dummy.

Dad keeps all of the dummies in good shape. He calls the attic his Dummy Museum. Spread around the room are a dozen old ventriloquist's dummies that he has collected.

He spends all his spare time fixing them up. Painting them. Giving them fresh wigs. Making new suits and trousers for them. Working on their insides, making sure their eyes and mouths move correctly.

These days, Dad doesn't get to use his ventriloquist skills very often. Sometimes he'll take one of the dummies to a kid's birthday party and put on a show. Sometimes people in town will invite him to perform at a party to raise money for a school or library.

But most of the time the dummies just sit up here, staring at each other.

Some of them are propped against the attic wall. Some are sprawled out on the couch. Some of them sit in folding chairs, hands crossed in their laps. Wilbur is the only one lucky enough to have his own armchair.

When Dan and I were little, we were afraid to come up to the attic. I didn't like the way the dummies stared at me. I thought their grins were evil.

Dan liked to stick his hand into their backs and move their mouths. He made the dummies say frightening things.

"I'm going to get you, Trina!" he would make Rocky growl. Rocky is the mean-faced dummy that sneers instead of smiles. He's dressed like a tough guy in a red-and-white striped T-shirt and black jeans. He's really evil-looking. *"I'm coming to your room tonight, Trina. And I'm going to GET you!"*

"Stop it, Dan! Stop it!" I would scream. Then I would go running downstairs and tell Mum that Dan was scaring me.

I was only eight or nine.

I'm a lot older now. And braver. But I still feel a little creeped out when I come up here.

I know it's stupid. But sometimes I imagine the dummies sitting around up here, talking to each other, giggling and laughing.

7

Sometimes late at night when I'm lying in bed, the ceiling creaks over my head. Footsteps! I picture the dummies walking around in the attic, their heavy black shoes clonking over the floorboards.

I picture them wrestling around on the old couch. Or playing a wild game of catch, their wooden hands snapping as they catch the ball.

Stupid? Of course it's stupid.

But I can't help it.

They're supposed to be funny little guys. But they scare me.

I hate the way they stare at me without blinking. And I hate the red-lipped grins frozen on their faces.

Dan and I come up to the attic because Dan likes to play with them. And because I like to see how Dad fixes them up.

But I really don't like to come up to the attic alone.

Dan picked up Miss Lucy. That's the only girl dummy in the group. She has curly blonde hair and bright blue eyes.

My brother stuck his hand into the dummy's back and perched her on his knee. "Hi, Trina," he made the dummy say in a high, shrill voice.

Dan started to make her say something else. But he stopped suddenly. His mouth dropped open—like a dummy's—and he pointed across the room.

8

"Trina—l-look!" Dan stammered. "Over there!"

I turned quickly. And I saw Rocky, the mean-looking dummy, blink his eyes.

I gasped as the dummy leaned forward and sneered. *"Trina, I'm going to GET you!"* he growled.

I uttered a startled cry and jumped back.

I swung around, ready to run to the attic steps—and I saw Dan laughing.

"Hey—!" I cried out angrily. "What's going on here?"

I turned back to see Dad climb to his feet behind Rocky's chair. He carried Rocky in one arm. Dad's grin was as wide as a dummy's!

"Gotcha!" he cried in Rocky's voice.

I turned angrily on my brother. "Did you know Dad was back there? Did you know Dad was here the whole time?"

Dan nodded. "Of course."

"You two are both dummies!" I cried. I flung my red hair back with both hands and let out an exasperated sigh. "That was so stupid!"

"You fell for it," Dan shot back, grinning at Dad.

"Who's the dummy here?" Dad made Rocky say. "Hey—who's pulling *your* string? I'm not a dummy—touch wood!"

Dan laughed, but I just shook my head.

Dad refused to give up. "Hey—come over here!" he made Rocky say. "Scratch my back. I think I've got termites!"

I gave in and laughed. I'd heard that joke a million times. But I knew Dad wouldn't stop trying until I laughed.

He's a really good ventriloquist. You can never see his lips move. But his jokes are totally lame.

I suppose that's why he had to give up the act and open a camera shop. I don't know for sure. It all happened before I was born.

Dad set Rocky back on his chair. The dummy sneered up at us. Such a bad-news dummy. Why couldn't he smile like the others?

Dad pushed his glasses up on his nose. "Come over here," he said. "I want to show you something."

He put one hand on my shoulder and one hand on Dan's shoulder and led us to the other end of the big attic room. This is where Dad has his workshop—his worktable and all his tools and supplies for fixing up the dummies.

Dad reached under the worktable and pulled up a large brown-paper shopping bag. I could tell by the smile on his face what he had in the bag. But I didn't say anything to ruin his surprise.

Slowly, carefully, Dad reached into the shopping bag. His smile grew wider as he lifted out a dummy. "Hey, guys—check this out!" Dad exclaimed.

The dummy had been folded up inside the bag. Dad set it down flat on the worktable and carefully unfolded the arms and legs. He looked like a surgeon starting an operation.

"I found this one in a rubbish bin," he told us. "Do you believe someone just threw it away?"

He tilted the dummy up so we could see it. I followed Dan up to the worktable to get a better look.

"The head was split in two," Dad said, placing one hand at the back of the dummy's neck. "But it took two seconds to repair it. Just a little glue."

I leaned close to check out Dad's new treasure. It had wavy brown hair painted on top of its head. The face was kind of strange. Kind of intense.

The eyes were bright blue. They shimmered. Sort of like real eyes. The dummy had bright red painted lips, curved up into a smile.

An ugly smile, I thought. Kind of gross and nasty.

His lower lip had a chip on one side so that it didn't quite match the other lip.

The dummy wore a grey double-breasted suit over a white shirt collar. The collar was stapled to his neck.

He didn't have a shirt. Instead, his wooden

chest had been painted white. Big black leather shoes—very scuffed up—dangled from his skinny grey trouser legs.

"Can you believe someone just threw him away?" Dad repeated. "Isn't he great?"

"Yeah. Great," I murmured. I didn't like the new dummy at all. I didn't like his face, the way his blue eyes gleamed, the crooked smile.

Dan must have felt the same way. "He's kind of tough-looking," he said. He picked up one of the dummy's wooden hands. It had deep scratches all over it. The knuckles appeared cut and bruised. As if the dummy had been in a fight.

"Not as tough-looking as Rocky over there," Dad replied. "But he does have a strange smile." He picked at the small chip in the dummy's lip. "I can fill that in with some liquid wood filler. Then I'll give the whole face a fresh paint job."

"What's the dummy's name?" I asked.

Dad shrugged. "Beats me. Maybe we'll call him Smiley."

"Smiley?" I made a disgusted face.

Dad started to reply. But the phone rang downstairs. One ring. Two. Three.

"I suppose your mum is still at that school meeting," Dad said. He ran to the stairs. "I'd better answer it. Don't touch Smiley till I get back." He vanished down the stairs.

I picked up the dummy's head carefully in

13

both hands. "Dad did a great gluing job," I said.

"He should do *your* head next!" Dan shot back.

Typical.

"I don't think Smiley is a good name for him," Dan said, slapping the dummy's hands together.

"How about Dan Junior?" I suggested. "Or Dan the Third?"

He ignored me. "How many dummies does Dad have now?" He turned back towards the others across the attic and quickly counted them.

I counted faster. "This new one makes thirteen," I said.

Dan's eyes went wide. "Wow. That's an unlucky number."

"Well, if we count you, it's fourteen!" I said.

Gotcha, Danny Boy!

Dan stuck out his tongue at me. He set the dummy's hands down on its chest. "Hey—what's that?" He reached into the pocket of the grey suit jacket and pulled out a folded-up slip of paper.

"Maybe that has the dummy's name on it," I said. I grabbed the paper out of Dan's hands and raised it to my face. I unfolded it and started to read.

"Well?" Dan tried to grab it back. But I swung out of his reach. "What's the name?"

"It doesn't say," I told him. "There are just these weird words. Foreign, I think."

I moved my lips silently as I struggled to read them. Then I read the words out loud: *"Karru marri odonna loma molonu karrano."*

Dan's mouth dropped open. "Huh? What's *that* supposed to mean?" he cried.

He grabbed the paper from my hand. "I think you read it upside down!"

"No way!" I protested.

I glanced down at the dummy.

The glassy blue eyes stared up at me.

Then the right eye slowly closed. The dummy *winked* at me.

And then his left hand shot straight up—and slapped me in the face.

"Hey—!" I shouted. I jerked back as pain shot through my jaw.

"What's your problem?" Dan demanded, glancing up from the slip of paper.

"Didn't you *see*?" I shrieked. "He—he *slapped* me!" I rubbed my cheek.

Dan rolled his eyes. "Yeah. Sure."

"No—really!" I cried. "First he winked at me. Then he slapped me."

"Tell me another one," Dan groaned. "You're such a jerk, Trina. Just because you fall for Dad's jokes doesn't mean I'm going to fall for yours."

"But I'm telling the truth!" I insisted.

I glanced up to see Dad poke his head up at the top of the stairs. "What's going on, guys?"

Dan folded up the slip of paper and tucked it back into the dummy's jacket pocket. "Nothing much," he told Dad.

"Dad—the new dummy!" I cried, still rubbing my aching jaw. "He *slapped* me!"

16

Dad laughed. "Sorry, Trina. You'll have to do better than that. You can't kid a kidder."

That's one of Dad's favourite expressions: "You can't kid a kidder."

"But, Dad—" I stopped. I could see he wasn't going to believe me. I wasn't even sure I believed it myself.

I glanced down at the dummy. He stared blankly up at the ceiling. Totally lifeless.

"I have news, guys," Dad said, sitting the new dummy up. "That was my brother—your uncle Cal—on the phone. He's coming for a short visit while Aunt Susan's away on business. And he's bringing your cousin Zane with him. It's Zane's spring vacation from school, too."

Dan and I both groaned. Dan stuck his finger in his mouth and pretended to puke.

Zane isn't our favourite cousin.

He's our *only* cousin.

He's twelve, but you'd think he was five or six. He's pretty nerdy. His nose runs a lot. And he's kind of a wimp.

Kind of a *major* wimp.

"Hey, stop groaning," Dad scolded. "Zane is your only cousin. He's family."

Dan and I groaned again. We couldn't help it.

"He isn't a bad kid," Dad continued, narrowing his eyes at us behind his glasses. That meant he was being serious. "You two have to promise me something."

17

"What kind of promise?" I asked.

"You have to promise me that you'll be nicer to Zane this time."

"We were nice to him last time," Dan insisted. "We *talked* to him, didn't we?"

"You scared him to death last time," Dad said, frowning. "You made him believe that this old house is haunted. And you scared him so badly, he ran outside and refused to come back in."

"Dad, it was all a joke," I protested.

"Yeah. It was a scream!" Dan agreed. He poked me in the side with his elbow. "A scream. Get it?"

"Not funny," Dad said unhappily. "Not funny at all. Listen, guys—Zane can't help it if he's a little timid. He'll outgrow it. You just have to be nice to him."

Dan sniggered. "Zane is afraid of your dummies, Dad. Can you believe it?"

"Then don't drag him up here and scare the life out of him," Dad ordered.

"How about if we just play one or two little jokes on him?" Dan asked.

"No tricks," Dad replied firmly. "None."

Dan and I exchanged glances.

"Promise me," Dad insisted. "I mean it. Right now. Both of you. Promise me there will be no tricks. Promise me you won't try to scare your cousin."

18

"Okay. I promise," I said. I raised my right hand as if I were swearing an oath.

"I promise, too," Dan said softly.

I checked to see if his fingers were crossed. They weren't.

Dan and I had both made a solemn promise. We both promised not to terrify our cousin. And we meant it.

But it was a promise we couldn't keep.

Before the week was over, our cousin Zane would be terrified.

And so would we.

I was playing the piano when Zane arrived. The piano is tucked away in a small room at the back of the house. It's a small black upright piano, kind of worn and scratched. Dad bought it from my old music teacher who moved to Cleveland.

Two of the pedals don't work. And the piano really needs to be tuned. But I love to play it— especially when I'm stressed out or excited. It always helps to calm me down.

I'm pretty good at it. Even Dan agrees. Most of the time he pushes me off the piano bench so he can play "Chopsticks". But sometimes he stands beside me and listens. I've been practising some nice Haydn pieces and some of the easy Chopin *etudes*.

Anyway, I was in the back of the house banging away on the piano when Zane and Uncle Cal arrived. I suppose I was a little nervous about seeing Zane again.

Dan and I were really mean to him during his

last visit. Like Dad said, Zane has always been scared of this old house. And we did everything we could to make him even *more* scared.

We walked around in the attic every night, howling softly like ghosts, making the floor creak. We crept into his bedroom wardrobe in the middle of the night and made him think his clothes were dancing. We hung up a pair of Mum's tights so they cast a ghostly shadow of legs on to his bedroom floor.

Poor Zane. I think Dan and I went a little too far. After a few days, he jumped at every sound. And his eyes kept darting from side to side like a frightened lizard's.

I heard him tell Uncle Cal that he never wanted to come back here.

Dan and I laughed about that. But it wasn't very nice.

So I was a little nervous about seeing Zane again. I was playing the piano so loudly, I didn't hear the doorbell. Dan had to come running in and tell me Uncle Cal and Zane had arrived.

I jumped up from the piano bench. "How does Zane look?" I asked my brother.

"Big," Dan replied. "He's grown a lot. And he's let his hair grow long."

Zane was always a pretty big guy. That's why Dan and I thought his being a total wimp was so funny.

21

He's big and beefy. Not tall. He's built kind of like a bulldog. A big blond bulldog.

I guess he's actually good-looking. He has round blue eyes, wavy blond hair, and a nice smile. He looks as if he works out or plays sports. He really doesn't look like the wimp type at all.

That's why it's such a riot to see him quivering in fear. Or wailing like a baby. Running to his mum or dad in terror.

I followed Dan through the back hall. "Did Zane say anything to you?" I asked.

"Just hi," Dan replied.

"A friendly 'hi' or an unfriendly 'hi'?" I demanded.

Dan didn't have time to answer. We had reached the front hall.

"Hey—!" Uncle Cal greeted me, stretching out his arms for a hug. Uncle Cal looks a lot like a chipmunk. He's very small. He has a round face, a twitchy little nose, and two teeth that poke out from his upper lip.

"You're getting so tall!" he exclaimed as I hugged him. "You've grown a lot, Trina!"

Why do grown-ups *always* have to comment on how tall kids are getting? Can't they think of anything else to say?

I saw Dad lugging their two heavy suitcases up the stairs.

"I didn't know if you'd be hungry or not," Mum

told Uncle Cal. "So I made a lot of sand-wiches."

I turned to say hi to Zane. And a flash of white light made me cry out in surprise.

"Don't move. One more," I heard Zane say.

I blinked rapidly, trying to clear the light from my eyes. When I finally focused, I saw that Zane had a camera up to his face.

He clicked it. Another bright flash of light.

"That's good," he said. "You looked really surprised. I only like to take candid shots."

"Zane is really into photography," Uncle Cal said, grinning proudly.

"I'm blind!" I cried, rubbing my eyes.

"I needed extra flash because this house is so dark," Zane said. He lowered his head to the camera and fiddled with his lens.

Dad came shuffling down the stairs. Zane turned and snapped his picture.

"Zane is really into photography," Uncle Cal repeated to my father. "I told him maybe you've got an old camera or two at the shop that he could have."

"Uh . . . maybe," Dad replied.

Uncle Cal makes a lot more money than Dad. But whenever he visits, he always tries to get Dad to give him stuff.

"Nice camera," Dad told Zane. "What kind of photos do you like to take?"

"Candid shots," Zane replied, pushing back

his blond hair. "And I take a lot of still lifes." He stepped into the hall and flashed a close-up of the banister.

Dan leaned close and whispered in my ear, "He's still a pain. Let's give him a really good scare."

"No way!" I whispered back. "No scares this time. We promised Dad—remember?"

"I've set up a darkroom in the basement," Dad told Zane. "Sometimes I bring developing work home from the shop. You can use the darkroom this week, if you want to."

"Great!" Zane replied.

"I told Zane maybe you have some sheets of developing paper you can spare," Uncle Cal said to Dad.

Zane raised his camera and flashed another picture. Then he turned to Dan. "Are you still into video games?" he asked.

"Yeah," Dan replied. "Mostly sports games. I have the new *NBA Jams*. And I'm saving my allowance to get the new thirty-two-bit system. You still play?"

Zane shook his head. "Not since I got my camera. I don't really have time for games any more."

"How about some sandwiches, everyone?" Mum asked, moving towards the dining room.

"I think I'd like to unpack first," Uncle Cal told her. "Zane, you should unpack, too."

We all split up. Dan and Dad disappeared somewhere. Uncle Cal and Zane went up to their rooms to unpack—our big old house has a lot of extra bedrooms.

I was going into the kitchen to help Mum with the sandwiches when I heard Zane scream.

A shrill scream from upstairs.

A scream of horror.

Mum gasped and dropped the sandwich tray she was carrying.

I spun around and went running to the front hall.

Dad was already halfway up the stairs. "What's wrong?" he called. "Zane—what's the matter?"

When I reached the first floor, I saw Dan step out of his room. Zane stood in the hallway. Someone lay stretched across the floor at his feet.

Even from halfway down the hall, I could see that Zane was trembling.

I hurried over to him.

Who was sprawled on the floor like that, legs and arms all twisted?

"Zane—what happened? What happened?" Dad and Uncle Cal both shouted.

Zane stood there shaking all over. The camera seemed to tremble, too, swinging on its strap over his chest.

I glanced down at the body on the floor.

A ventriloquist's dummy.

Rocky.

Rocky sneered up at the ceiling. His red-and-white striped shirt had rolled up halfway, revealing his wooden body. One leg was bent under him. Both arms were stretched out over the floor.

"That d-dummy—" Zane stammered, pointing down at Rocky. "It—it *fell* on me when I opened the bedroom door."

"Huh? It *what*?" Uncle Cal cried.

"It dropped down on me," Zane repeated. "When I pushed the door. I didn't mean to scream. It just scared me, that's all. It was so heavy. And it fell near my head."

I turned and saw Dad glaring angrily at Dan.

Dan raised both hands in protest. "Hey—don't look at *me*!" he cried.

"Dan, you made a promise," Dad said sharply.

"I didn't do it!" Dan cried. "It had to be Trina!"

"Hey—no way!" I protested. "No way! I didn't do it!"

Dad narrowed his eyes at me. "I suppose the dummy climbed up on top of the door by himself!" he said, rolling his eyes.

"It was just a joke," Uncle Cal chimed in. "You're okay—right, Zane?"

"Yeah. Sure." Zane's cheeks were red. I could see he was embarrassed by all the fuss. "I just

27

wasn't expecting something to fall on me. You know." He stared at the floor.

"Let's finish unpacking," Uncle Cal suggested. "I'm starting to get hungry." He turned to Dad. "Do you have any extra pillows? There's only one on my bed. And I like to sleep with a *lot* of pillows."

"I'll see if we have any more," Dad replied. He frowned at me. "You and Dan—take Rocky up to the attic. And no more little jokes. You promised—remember?"

I picked Rocky up carefully and slung him over my shoulder. "Get the attic door for me," I instructed Dan.

We made our way down the hall. "What is your problem, Mouse?" I whispered to my brother.

"Don't call me Mouse," he replied through gritted teeth. "You know I hate it."

"Well, I hate broken promises," I told him. "You can't wait one minute to start scaring Zane? You're going to get us in major trouble."

"Me?" Dan put on his innocent act. "I didn't hide the dummy up there. *You* did—and you know it!"

"Did not!" I whispered angrily.

"Hey, guys, can I come with you?" I turned to see Zane right behind us. I hadn't realized he'd followed us.

"You want to come up to the Dummy

Museum?" I asked, unable to hide my surprise. Last visit, Zane had been afraid of the dummies.

"Yeah. I want to take some pictures," he replied. He raised his camera in both hands.

"Cool," Dan said. "That's a cool idea." I could see that he was trying to be friendly to Zane.

I didn't want to be left out. "It's good that you're into photography," I told Zane.

"Yeah. I know," he replied.

Dan led the way up the attic stairs. Halfway up, I turned back. I saw Zane lingering at the bottom.

"Are you coming up or not?" I called down. My voice echoed in the narrow, dark stairwell.

I caught a look of fear on Zane's face. He was trying to be brave, I realized. Trying not to be afraid the way he was last time.

"Coming," he called up. I saw him take a deep breath. Then he came running up the stairs.

He stayed close to Dan and me as we crossed the attic. The eyes peered out at us darkly from around the big room.

I clicked on the light. The dummies all came into view. Propped on chairs and the old couch, leaning against the wall, they grinned at us.

I carried Rocky over to his folding chair. I slid him off my shoulder and set him down. I crossed his arms in his lap and straightened his striped shirt. The mean-looking dummy sneered up at me.

"Uncle Danny has a few new guys," Zane said from across the room. He stood close to Dan in front of the couch. He held the camera in his hands, but he didn't take any pictures. "Where does he find them?"

"He found the newest one in a rubbish bin," I replied, pointing to the mean-looking dummy.

Dan picked up Miss Lucy and held it up to Zane. "Hiya, Zane! Take my picture!" Dan made Miss Lucy say in a high, shrill voice.

Zane obediently raised the camera to his eye. "Say cheese," he told Miss Lucy.

"Cheese," Dan said in Miss Lucy's high voice.

Zane flashed a picture.

"Give me a big wet kiss!" Dan made Miss Lucy say. He shoved the dummy's face close to Zane's.

Zane backed away. "Yuck."

"Put the dummy down," I told my brother. "We'd better get back downstairs. They're all probably waiting for us."

"Okay, okay," Dan grumbled. He turned to set Miss Lucy down. Zane wandered down the row of dummies, studying them.

I bent down and straightened Wilbur's bow-tie. The old dummy was starting to look really ragged.

I was still working on the bow-tie when I heard a hard *slap*.

And I heard Zane's startled cry of pain.

"Owwww!"

I spun around and saw Zane rubbing his jaw.

"Hey—that dummy *slapped* me!" he cried angrily.

He pointed to a red-haired dummy on the arm of the couch.

"I-I don't *believe* it!" Zane exclaimed. "It swung its arm up, and it—it *slapped* me!"

Dan stood behind the couch. I saw a smile spread over his face. Then he burst out laughing. "Get serious," he told Zane. "That's impossible."

"You did it!" Zane accused my brother, still rubbing his jaw. "You moved the dummy!"

"No way!" Dan backed away till he bumped the wall. "How could I? I was behind the couch the whole time."

I stepped quickly up to the couch. "Which dummy was it?" I demanded.

Zane pointed to a dummy with red hair and bright red freckles painted all over his grinning face. "That guy."

"Arnie," I reported. "One of Dad's first dummies."

"I don't care what his name is," Zane snapped. "He slapped me!"

"But that's stupid," I insisted. "It's just a ventriloquist's dummy, Zane. Here. Look."

I picked Arnie up. The old dummy was heavier than I remembered. I started to hand him to Zane. But my cousin backed away.

"Something weird is going on here," Zane said, keeping his eyes on the dummy. "I'm going to tell Uncle Danny."

"No. Don't tell Dad," I pleaded. "Give me a break, Zane. It'll get us in big trouble."

"Yeah. Don't tell," Dan chimed in. "The dummy probably just slipped or something. You know. It fell over."

"It reached up," Zane insisted. "I saw it swing its arm and—"

He was interrupted by Mum's voice from downstairs. "Hurry up, kids. Get down here. We're all waiting for you."

"Coming!" I shouted. I dropped Arnie back on to the arm of the couch. He fell into the dummy next to him. I left him like that and followed Dan and Zane to the stairs.

I held Dan back and let Zane go down by himself. "What are you trying to prove?" I angrily asked my brother. "That wasn't funny."

"Trina, I didn't do it. I swear!" Dan claimed, raising his right hand. "I swear!"

"So what are you saying?" I demanded. "That the dummy really reached up and slapped him?"

Dan twisted his face. He shrugged. "I don't know. I just know that I didn't do it. I didn't swing that dummy's arm."

"Don't be stupid," I replied. "Of course you did." I shoved my brother towards the stairs.

"Hey—give me a break," he muttered.

"You're a total liar," I told him. "You think you can scare Zane—and me. But it isn't worth it, Dan. We promised Dad, remember? Remember?"

He ignored me and started down the stairs.

I felt really angry. I knew that Dan had perched the dummy on top of the bedroom door so that it would fall on Zane. And I knew that he had swung the dummy's arm to slap Zane.

I wondered how far Dan would go to frighten our cousin.

I knew I had to stop him. If Dan kept this up, he'd get us both grounded for life. Or worse.

But what could I do?

I was still thinking about it in bed later that night. I couldn't get to sleep. I lay there, staring up at the ceiling, thinking about Dan and what a liar he was.

Dummies are made of wood and cloth, I told

myself. They don't swing their arms and slap people.

And they don't get up and walk around the house and climb up on to doors on their own. They don't walk on their own. . .

They don't. . .

I finally started to drift off to sleep when I heard light footsteps on my bedroom carpet.

And then a hoarse whisper close to my ear: *"Trina . . . Trina. . ."*

"Trina . . . Trina. . ."

The hoarse whisper—so near my ear—made me shoot straight up in bed.

I leaped to my feet. Pulled the covers with me. Lurched forward.

And nearly knocked Zane on to his back.

"Zane?"

He stumbled backwards. "Sorry!" he whispered. "I thought you were awake."

"Zane!" I repeated. My heart thudded in my chest. "What are you *doing* in here?"

"Sorry," he whispered, backing up some more. He stopped a few centimetres in front of my dressing-table. "I didn't mean to scare you. I just—"

I held my hand over my heart. I could feel it start to slow back down to normal. "Sorry I jumped out at you like that," I told him. "I was half asleep, I guess. And when you whispered my name. . ."

I clicked on the bed-table lamp. I rubbed my eyes and squinted at Zane.

He was wearing baggy blue pyjamas. One pyjama leg had rolled up nearly to his knee. His blond hair had fallen over his face. He had such a frightened, little-boy expression on his face. He looked about six years old!

"I tried to wake up Dad," he whispered. "But he's such a sound sleeper. I kept knocking on his bedroom door and calling to him. But he didn't hear me. So I came in here."

"What's your problem?" I asked, stretching my arms over my head.

"I-I heard voices," he stammered, glancing to the open bedroom door.

"Excuse me? Voices?" I pushed my hair back. Straightened my long nightshirt. Studied him.

He nodded. "I heard voices. Upstairs. I mean, I *think* they were upstairs. Funny voices. Talking very fast."

I squinted at him. "You heard voices in the *attic*?"

He nodded again. "Yeah. I'm pretty sure."

"I'm pretty sure you were dreaming," I sighed. I shook my head.

"No. I was wide awake. Really." He picked up a little stuffed bear from my dressing-table. He squeezed it between his hands.

"I never sleep very well in new places," he told me. "I *never* sleep very well in this house!" He let out an unhappy laugh. "I was wide awake."

"There's no one in the attic," I said, yawning. I tilted my ear to the ceiling. "Listen," I instructed. "Silent up there. No voices."

We both listened to the silence for a while.

Then Zane put down the stuffed bear. "Do you think I could have a bowl of cereal?" he asked.

"Huh?" I gaped at him.

"A bowl of cereal always helps calm me down," he said. An embarrassed smile crossed his face. "Just a habit from when I was a kid."

I squinted at my clock radio. It was a little after midnight. "You want a bowl of cereal *now*?"

He nodded. "Is that okay?" he asked shyly.

Poor guy, I thought. He's really freaked out.

"Sure," I said. "I'll come down to the kitchen with you. Show you where everything is."

I found my flip-flops and slipped my feet into them. I keep them under my bed. I don't like walking barefoot on the floorboards in the hall. There are a lot of nails that poke up from the floor.

Mum and Dad keep saying they're going to buy a carpet. But money is tight. I don't think a carpet is top of their list.

Zane appeared a little calmer. I smiled at him and led the way into the hall.

He's not such a bad guy, I thought. He's a little wimpy—but so what? I decided to have a serious talk with Dan first thing in the morning.

I planned to make Dan *promise* he wouldn't pull any more scares on Zane.

The long hall was so dark, Zane and I both held on to the wall as we made our way to the stairs. Mum and Dad used to keep a little night-light at the end of the hall. But the bulb burned out, and they never replaced it.

Holding on to the banister, we made our way slowly down the steps. Pale light from outside cast long blue shadows over the living room. In the dim light, our old furniture rose up like ghosts around the room.

"This house always creeps me out," Zane whispered, staying close by my side as we crossed through the front room.

"I've lived here all my life, and sometimes I'm scared of it, too," I confessed. "Old houses make so many strange sounds. Sometimes I think I hear the house groaning and moaning."

"I really did hear voices," Zane whispered.

We crept through the shadows to the kitchen. My flip-flops slapped on the lino. Silvery moon-light washed through the curtains over the kitchen window.

I started to fumble on the wall for the light switch.

But I stopped when I saw the dark figure slumped at the kitchen table.

Zane saw him, too. I heard Zane gasp. He jerked back into the doorway.

"Dad? Are you still up?" I called. "Why are you sitting in the dark?"

My hand found the light switch. I clicked on the kitchen light.

And Zane and I both let out a scream.

I recognized the red-and-white striped shirt. I didn't even have to see the face.

Rocky leaned over the table, his wooden head propped in his hands.

Zane and I crept closer to the table. I moved to the other side. The dummy sneered at me. His glassy eyes were cold and cruel.

Such a nasty expression.

"How did *he* get down here?" Zane asked. He stared hard at the dummy, as if expecting the dummy to answer.

"Only one way," I murmured. "He sure didn't walk."

Zane turned to me. "You mean Dan?"

I sighed. "Of course. Who else? Mister Stupid Jokes."

"But how did your brother know we'd be coming down to the kitchen tonight?" Zane asked.

"Let's go and ask him," I replied.

I knew Dan was awake. Probably sitting on the edge of his bed, waiting eagerly to hear us scream from the kitchen. Giggling to himself. So pleased with himself.

So pleased that he broke his promise to Dad. And gave Zane and me a little scare.

I clenched both hands into tight fists. I could feel the anger rising in my chest.

When I get really furious like that, I usually go to the back room and pound the piano. I pound out a Sousa march or a hard, fast rock song. I pound the keys till I start to calm down.

Tonight, I decided, I would pound my brother instead.

"Come on," I urged Zane. "Upstairs."

I took one last glance at Rocky, slouched over the kitchen table. The dummy stared blankly back at me.

I really hate that dummy, I thought. I'm going to ask Dad to put him away in a cupboard or a trunk.

I forced myself to turn away from the sneering, wooden face. Then I put both hands on Zane's shoulders and guided him back to the stairs.

"I'm going to tell Dan that we're both fed up with his stupid jokes," I whispered to my cousin. "Enough is enough. We'll make him promise to stop leaving that dummy everywhere we go."

Zane didn't reply. In the dim light, I could see the grim expression on his face.

I wondered what he was thinking about. Was he remembering his last visit to our house? Was he remembering how Dan and I terrified him then?

Maybe he doesn't trust me, either, I told myself.

We climbed the stairs and crept down the dark hallway to my brother's room.

The door was half open. I pushed it open the rest of the way and stepped inside. Zane kept close behind me.

I expected Dan to be sitting up, waiting for us. I expected to see him grinning, enjoying his little joke.

Silvery moonlight flooded in through his double windows. From the doorway, I could see him clearly. Lying on his side in bed. Covers up to his chin. Eyes tightly closed.

Was he faking? Was he really awake?

"Dan," I whispered. "Da-an."

He didn't move. His eyes didn't open.

"Dan—I'm coming to *tickle* you!" I whispered. He could never keep a straight face when I threatened him. Dan is *very* ticklish.

But he didn't move.

Zane and I crept closer. Up to the bed. We both stood over my brother, staring hard at him, studying him in the silvery light.

He was breathing softly, in a steady rhythm. His mouth was open a little. He made short whistling sounds. Mouse sounds. With his pointy chin and upturned nose, he really did look like a little mouse.

I leaned over him. "Da-an, get ready to be tickled!" I whispered.

I leaned back, expecting him to leap out at me, to shout "Boo!" or something.

But he continued sleeping, whistling softly with each breath.

I turned to Zane, who hung back in the centre of the room. "He's really asleep," I reported.

"Let's go back to our rooms," Zane replied in a soft whisper. He yawned.

I followed him to the bedroom door. "What about your cereal?" I asked.

"Forget it. I'm too sleepy now."

We were nearly at the door when I heard someone move in the hall.

"Ohhh." I let out a low moan as a face appeared in the doorway.

Rocky's face.

He had followed us upstairs!

I grabbed Zane's arm. We both shouted cries of surprise.

The dummy moved quickly into the room.

I cut my cry short as I saw that he wasn't walking on his own. He was being carried.

Dad had the dummy by the back of the neck.

"Hey—what's going on?" Dan called sleepily from behind us. He raised his head from the pillow and squinted at us. "Huh? What's everybody doing in my room?"

"That's what *I'd* like to know," Dad said sharply. He gazed suspiciously from Zane to me.

"You—you woke me up," Dan murmured. He cleared his throat. Then he propped himself up on one elbow. "Why are you carrying that dummy, Dad?"

"Perhaps one of you would like to answer that question," Dad growled. He had pulled a robe over his pyjamas. His hair was matted to his forehead. He wasn't wearing his glasses, so he squinted at us.

"What's going on? I don't understand," Dan said sleepily. He rubbed his eyes.

Was he putting on an act? I wondered. His innocent-little-boy act?

"I heard noises downstairs," Dad said, shifting Rocky to his other hand. "I went down to see what was going on. I found this dummy sitting at the kitchen table."

"I didn't put him there!" Dan cried, suddenly wide awake. "Really. I didn't!"

"Neither did Zane or me!" I chimed in.

Dad turned to me. He sighed. "I'm really sleepy. I don't like these jokes in the middle of the night."

"But I didn't do it!" I cried.

Dad squinted hard at me. He really couldn't see at all without his glasses. "Do I have to punish you and your brother?" he demanded. "Do I have to ground you? Or keep you from going away to camp this summer?"

"*No!*" Dan and I both cried at once. Dan and I were both going to summer camp for the first time this year. It's all we've talked about since Christmas.

"Dad, I was asleep. Really," Dan insisted.

"No more stories," Dad replied wearily. "The next time one of my dummies is somewhere he shouldn't be, you're both in major trouble."

"But, Dad—" I started.

"One last chance," Dad said. "I mean it. If I

45

see Rocky out of the attic again, you've both *had* it!" He waved Zane and me to the door. "Get to your rooms. Now. Not another word."

"Do you believe me or not?" Dan demanded.

"I don't believe that Rocky has been moving around the house on his own," Dad replied. "Now lie down and get back to sleep, Dan. I'm giving you one last chance. Don't blow it."

Dad followed Zane and me into the hall. "See you in the morning," he murmured. He made his way to the attic stairs to take Rocky back up to the Dummy Museum. I heard him muttering to himself all the way up the stairs.

I said good night to Zane and headed to my room. I felt sleepy and upset and worried and confused—all at once.

I knew that Dan *had* to be the one who kept springing Rocky on Zane. But why was he doing it? And would he quit now—before Dad grounded us or totally ruined our summer?

I fell asleep, still asking myself question after question.

The next morning, I woke up early. I pulled on jeans and a sweatshirt and hurried downstairs for breakfast.

And there sat Rocky at the kitchen table.

I peered around the kitchen. No one else around.

How lucky that I was the first one downstairs!

I grabbed Rocky up by the back of the neck. Then I tucked him under one arm and dragged him up to the attic as fast as I could.

When I returned to the kitchen a few moments later, Mum had already started breakfast.

Phew! A close call.

"Trina—you're up early," Mum said, filling the coffee maker with water. "Are you okay?"

I glanced at the table. I had the sick feeling that Rocky would be sitting there sneering at me.

But of course he was upstairs in the attic. I had just carried him up there.

The table stood empty.

"I'm fine," I told her. "Just fine."

It was definitely Be Kind to Zane Day.

After breakfast, Dad hurried off to the camera

shop. A short while later, Mum and Uncle Cal left for the mall to do some shopping.

It was a bright morning. Yellow sunlight streamed in through the windows. The sky stretched clear and cloudless.

Zane brought down his camera. He decided it was a perfect day to take some photographs.

Dan and I expected him to go outside. But our cousin wanted to stay indoors and shoot.

"I'm very interested in mouldings," he told us.

We followed him around the house. Dan and I had made a solemn vow to be nice to Zane and not to scare him.

After breakfast, when Zane was upstairs getting his camera, I grabbed my brother. I pinned him against the wall. "No tricks," I told him.

Dan tried to wriggle away. But I'm stronger than he is. I kept him pinned against the wall. "Raise your right hand and swear," I instructed him.

"Okay, okay." He gave in easily. He raised his right hand, and he repeated the vow I recited. "No tricks against Zane. No making fun of Zane. No dummies—*anywhere*!"

I let him go as Zane returned with his camera. "You have some awesome mouldings," Zane said, gazing up at the living room ceiling.

"Really?" I replied, trying to sound interested. What could be interesting about a moulding?

Zane tilted up his camera. He focused for what

seemed like hours. Then he clicked a photo of the moulding above the living room curtains.

"Do you have a ladder?" he asked Dan. "I'd really like to get a closer shot. I'm afraid my zoom lens will distort it."

And so Dan hurried off to the basement to get Zane a ladder.

I was proud of my brother. He didn't complain about having to go and get the ladder. And he'd lasted a whole ten minutes without cracking any moulding jokes or making fun of Zane.

Which wasn't easy.

I mean, what kind of a nerd thinks it's cool to take photos of ceilings and walls?

Meanwhile, we had no school, and it was the sunniest, warmest, most beautiful day of March outside. Almost like spring. And Dan and I were stuck holding the ladder for Zane so he could use his macro lens and get a really tight moulding shot.

"Awesome!" Zane declared, snapping a few more. "Awesome!"

He climbed down the ladder. He adjusted the lens. Fiddled with some other dials on the camera.

"Want to go outside or something?" I suggested.

He didn't seem to hear me. "I'd like to get a few more banister shots," he announced. "See the way the sunlight is pouring through the wooden bars? It makes a really interesting pattern on the wall."

I started to say something rude. But Dan caught my eye. He shook a finger at me. A warning.

I bit my lip and didn't say anything.

This is sooooo boring, I thought. But at least we're keeping out of trouble.

We stood beside Zane as he photographed the banister from all angles. After about the tenth shot, his camera began to hum and whir.

"End of the roll," he announced. His eyes lit up. "Know what would be really cool? To go down into the basement to the darkroom and develop these right now."

"Cool," I replied. I tried to sound sincere. Dan and I were both trying so hard to be nice to this kid!

"Uncle Danny said I could use his darkroom downstairs," Zane said, watching the camera as it rewound the film roll. "That would be awesome."

"Awesome," I repeated.

Dan and I exchanged glances. The most beautiful day of the *century*—and we were going down to a dark closet in the basement.

"I've never watched pictures get developed," Dan told our cousin. "Can you show me how to do it?"

"It's pretty easy," Zane replied, following us

down the basement stairs. "Once you get the hang of the timing."

We made our way through the laundry room, past the boiler, to the darkroom against the far wall. We slipped inside, and I clicked on the special red light.

"Close the door tightly," Zane instructed. "We can't let in any light at all."

I double-checked the darkroom door. Then Zane set to work. He arranged the developing pans. He poured bottles of chemicals into the pans. He unspooled the film roll and began to develop.

I'd watched Dad do it a hundred times before. It really was kind of interesting. And it was cool when the image began to appear and then darken on the developing paper.

Dan and I stood close to Zane, watching him work.

"I think I got some very good angles on the living room mouldings," Zane said. He dipped the large sheet of paper in one pan. Then he pulled it up, let it drip for a few seconds, and lowered it into the pan beside it.

A grin spread over his face. "Let's take a look."

He leaned over the table. Raised the sheet of paper. Held it up to the red light.

His grin faded quickly. "Hey—who shot this?" he demanded angrily.

Dan and I moved closer to see the photo.

51

"Who shot this?" Zane repeated. He furiously picked up another sheet from the developing pan. Another one. Another one.

"How did these get on the roll?" he cried. He shoved them all towards Dan and me.

Photos of Rocky.

Close-up portraits.

Photo after photo of the sneering dummy.

"Who shot them? Who?" Zane demanded angrily, shoving the wet photos in our faces.

"I didn't!" Dan declared, pulling back.

"I didn't either!" I protested.

But then, who did? I asked myself, staring hard at the ugly, sneering face on each sheet.

Who did?

"What's going on up here, guys?"

The dummies stared back at me blankly. None of them replied.

"What's the story?" I demanded. My eyes moved from one dummy to the next. "Come on guys. Speak up or I'll come back here with an electric saw and give you all haircuts!"

Silence.

I paced back and forth in front of them, gazing at them sternly, my arms crossed in front of my chest.

It was late in the afternoon. The sun had begun to lower itself behind the trees. Orange light washed in through the dusty attic windows.

I had crept up to the attic to search for clues. Something weird was going on.

How did all those photos of Rocky get on to Zane's roll of film? Who took those photos?

The same person who kept carrying Rocky downstairs and sitting him where he would frighten Zane.

"It was Dan—right, guys?" I asked the wide-eyed dummies. "Dan came up here—right?"

I searched the floor. The couch. Under all the chairs.

I didn't find a single clue.

Now I was questioning the dummies. But of course they weren't being very helpful.

Stop wasting time and get back downstairs, I told myself.

I turned and started to the stairs—when I heard soft laughter.

"Huh?" I uttered a startled cry and spun around.

Another quiet laugh. A snigger.

And then a hoarse voice: *Is your hair red? Or are you starting to rust?*

"Excuse me?" I cried, raising a hand to my mouth. My eyes swept quickly from dummy to dummy.

Who said that?

"Hey, Trina—you're pretty. Pretty ugly!" That was followed by another soft snigger. Evil laughter.

"I like your perfume. What is it—flea and tick spray?"

My eyes stopped on the new dummy, the one Dad called Smiley. He sat straight up in the centre of the couch. The voice seemed to be coming from him.

"Pinch me. I'm having a nightmare. Or is that really your face?"

I froze. A cold shiver ran down my back.

The hoarse voice *did* come from the new dummy!

He stared blankly at me. His mouth hung open in a stiff, unpleasant grin.

But the voice came from Smiley. The rude insults came from Smiley.

But that's impossible! I told myself.

Impossible!

Ventriloquist's dummies can't talk without a ventriloquist.

"Th-this is crazy!" I stammered out loud.

And then the dummy started to move.

I let out a scream.

Dan popped up from behind the couch.

The dummy toppled on to its side.

"You-you-you—!" I spluttered, pointing furiously at my brother.

My heart was pounding. I felt cold all over. "That's not funny! You—you scared me to death!" I shrieked.

To my surprise, Dan didn't laugh. His eyes were narrowed. His mouth hung open. "Who was making those jokes?" he demanded. His eyes darted from dummy to dummy.

"Give me a break!" I shot back. "Are you going to tell me it wasn't you?"

He scratched his short brown hair. "I didn't say a word."

"Dan, you're the biggest liar!" I cried. "How long have you been up here? What are you doing here? You were spying on me—right?"

He shook his head and stepped out from

behind the couch. "What are *you* doing up here, Trina?" he asked. "Did you come up to get Rocky? To take Rocky downstairs again and try to scare Zane?"

I let out an angry growl and shoved Dan with all my might.

He stumbled backwards and fell on to the couch. He cried out as he landed on top of the new dummy. He and the dummy appeared to wrestle for a moment as Dan struggled to climb to his feet.

I stepped up close to the couch and blocked his way. As he tried to get up, I pushed him back down.

"You know I'm not the one who's been moving Rocky around," I shouted. "We all know *you've* been doing it, Dan. And you're going to get the two of us in real trouble with Dad."

"You're wrong!" Dan declared angrily. His little mouse face turned bright red. "Wrong! Wrong! Wrong!"

He burst up from the couch. The dummy bounced on the cushion. Its head turned. It appeared to grin up at me.

I turned to my brother. "If you weren't planning more trouble, what were you doing up here?"

"Waiting," he replied.

"Excuse me? Waiting for whom?" I demanded, crossing my arms over my chest.

"Just waiting," he insisted. "Don't you *get* it, Trina?"

I kicked at a ball of dust on the floor. It stuck to the toe of my trainer. "Get it? Get what?"

"Don't you see what's going on?" Dan demanded. "Haven't you caught on yet?"

I bent down and pulled the dust ball off my trainer. Now it stuck to my fingers. "What is in your little mouse brain?" I asked. I rolled my eyes. "This should be good."

My brother stepped up beside me. He lowered his voice to a whisper. "Zane is doing it all," he said.

I laughed. I wasn't sure I'd heard him.

"No. Really." He grabbed my arm. "I know I'm right, Trina. Zane is doing everything. Zane is moving the dummy, bringing it downstairs, then pretending to be scared. Zane made it slap him. Zane carried it to the kitchen table both of those times."

I shoved Dan's hand off my arm. Then I spread my hand over his forehead and pretended to check his temperature. "You are totally losing it," I told him. "Go and lie down. I'll tell Mum you're running a high fever."

"*Listen to me!*" Dan screeched. "I'm serious! I'm right. I know I'm right!"

"Why?" I demanded. "Why would Zane do that, Dan? Why would he scare himself?"

"To pay us back for last time," Dan replied.

"Don't you get it? Zane is trying to get us in trouble."

I dropped down on to the couch beside Smiley. I thought hard about what my brother was saying. "You mean Zane wants Dad to think that you and I are using the dummies to scare him."

"Yes!" Dan cried. "But Zane is doing it all. He's scaring himself. And making it look as if we're doing it—to get us in big trouble."

I fiddled with the dummy's hand as I thought about it some more. "Zane scare himself? I don't think so," I replied finally. "What gave you this idea? What proof do you have?"

Dan dropped down on the couch arm. "First of all," he started, "you didn't carry Rocky downstairs all those times, did you?"

I shook my head. "No way."

"Well, neither did I," Dan declared. "So who does that leave? Rocky isn't walking around by himself—right?"

"Of course not. But—"

"It was the camera that gave it away," Dan said. "The photos Zane developed of Rocky were the biggest clue."

I let the dummy hand fall to the couch. "What do you mean?" I asked. I really wasn't following my brother's thinking at all.

"That camera is never out of Zane's sight," Dan replied. "Most of the time, he keeps it around his neck. So who else could have snapped all those photos of Rocky?"

I swallowed hard. "You mean that Zane—?"

Dan nodded. "Zane was the only one who could have taken those pictures of Rocky. He sneaked up to the attic. He snapped them. Then he acted scared and angry when he developed them."

"But it was all an act?" I asked.

"Of course," Dan replied. "It's all been an act. To scare us. And to get us in trouble with Dad. Zane is trying to pay us back for how we scared him last time."

I still had my doubts. "It isn't like Zane," I argued. "He's so wimpy, so quiet and shy. He's not the kind of boy who plays tricks on people."

"He's had months to plan it!" Dan exclaimed. "Months to plan his revenge. We can prove it, Trina. We can hide up here and wait for him. That's why I was up here. Hiding behind the couch."

"To catch him in the act?"

Dan nodded. He whispered even though we were alone. "After everyone goes to bed tonight, let's sneak up here and wait. Wait and see if Zane comes."

"Okay," I agreed. "It's worth a try . . . I guess."

Was Dan right?

Would we catch Zane in the act?

I couldn't wait for everyone to go to sleep. I was dying to find out.

Gusts of wind rattled the attic windowpanes. Heavy clouds covered the moon.

We crept up the attic stairs into the darkness. Up a step. Then stop. Up a step. Then stop. Trying to be silent.

The old house moaned and groaned beneath us.

The attic stretched blacker than the stairway.

I reached for the light switch. But Dan slapped my hand away. "Are you crazy?" he whispered. "It has to be dark. Totally dark. Or else Zane will know that someone is up here."

"I know that," I whispered sleepily. "I just wanted to take one look at the dummies. You know. Make sure they're all here."

"They're all here," Dan replied impatiently. "Just keep moving. We'll hide behind the couch."

We crept on tiptoe over the attic floorboards. I couldn't see a thing. The heavy clouds kept any light from washing in through the windows.

Finally, my eyes adjusted to the darkness. I could see the arms of the couch. I saw dummy heads. Dummy shoulders. Shadows against shadows.

"Dan—where are you?" I whispered.

"Back here. Hurry." His whisper came from behind the couch.

I could feel the dummy eyes on me as I made my way around the couch. I thought I heard a soft snigger. The evil laughter again.

But that had to be my imagination.

I trailed my hand over the couch arm. Felt a wooden dummy hand resting on the arm. The dummy hand felt surprisingly warm.

Humanly warm.

Don't start imagining things, Trina, I scolded myself.

That dummy hand is warm because it's *hot* up in this attic.

The wind rattled the glass. Strong gusts roared against the roof, so low over our heads.

I heard a loud groan. A soft chuckle. A strange whistling sound.

Ignoring all the attic noises, I ducked down on the floor beside my brother. "Well? Here we are," I whispered. "Now what?"

"Sssshhhh." In the darkness, I could see him raise a finger to his lips. "Now we wait. And listen."

We both turned and rested our backs against

the back of the couch. I raised my knees and wrapped my arms around them.

"He isn't coming," I whispered. "This is a waste of time."

"Ssshhh. Just wait, Trina," Dan scolded. "Give him time."

I yawned. I felt so sleepy. The heat of the attic was making me even sleepier.

I shut my eyes and thought about Zane.

At dinner, he couldn't wait to pass around the photographs of Rocky. "I don't know who took these shots," Zane complained to my dad. "But they wasted half a roll of film."

Dad glared angrily at Dan and me. But he didn't make a fuss. "Can we talk about it after dinner?" he suggested quietly.

"I'm kind of scared," Zane told Dad in a trembling voice. "So many weird things have been happening. It's like the dummies have lives of their own." He shook his head. "Wow. I hope I don't have nightmares tonight."

"Let's not talk about the dummies now," Mum chimed in. "Zane, tell us about your school. Who is your teacher this year? What are you studying?"

"Could I have a second helping of potatoes?" Uncle Cal interrupted. He reached for the bowl. "They're so good. I may have to make a pig of myself."

Dad took another quick glance at the close-up

snapshots of Rocky. He flashed Dan and me another angry scowl. Then he set the photos down on the floor.

After dinner, Dan and I were careful to keep as far away from Dad as we could. There was no way we wanted to hear another lecture about how we were terrifying our poor cousin. And how we'd be punished if we didn't stop it at once.

Now it was a little before midnight. And we were huddled in the dark attic. Listening to the swirling wind and the moans and groans of the house. Backs pressed against the couch. Waiting. . .

I kept my eyes closed. Thinking hard. Thinking about Zane. About Rocky.

Dan and I aren't alone up here, I thought drowsily. There are thirteen wooden dummies up here with us. Thirteen pairs of eyes staring into the heavy darkness. Thirteen frozen grins. Except for Rocky's sneer, of course.

Empty, lifeless bodies. . .

Heavy, wooden heads and hands. . .

Thinking about the dummies, the dummies all around, I guess I drifted off to sleep.

Did I dream about the dummies?

Maybe I did.

I don't know how long I slept.

I was awakened by footsteps. Soft, shuffling footsteps across the attic floor.

And I knew the dummies had come alive.

I jerked my head up, listening hard.

My hands were still wrapped around my knees. Both hands had fallen asleep. They tingled. The back of my neck ached. My mouth felt dry and sour.

I uttered a silent gasp as I heard the shuffling, scraping footsteps move closer.

Not dummies walking around, I realized.

A single figure. One. One person. Moving slowly, carefully towards the couch.

Why did I think I'd heard dummies moving? It must have been a picture left over from my dream.

I shook my hands, trying to make them stop tingling.

I was wide awake now. Totally alert.

The footsteps scraped closer.

Could it be Dan? Where was Dan?

Had he climbed up while I slept? Was he making his way back to the couch?

No.

Squinting into the darkness, I saw Dan beside me.

He had climbed to his knees. He saw me move. He waved his hand and signalled for me to be silent.

Dan gripped the back of the couch with both hands. Then he leaned forward and peered out into the room.

I crawled to the other end of the couch. Then, keeping low, I poked my head out and squinted into the deep shadows. All greys and blacks.

The wind howled around the house. Across the big attic room, the windowpanes rattled and shook.

I wanted to jump out. To scream and jump out. And flash on the light.

But I felt Dan's hand on my arm. He must have read my thoughts. He raised a finger to his lips.

We both waited. Frozen there behind the couch. Crouching low. Listening to each footstep. Each creak of the floorboards.

The dark figure stopped in front of the folding chair next to the couch. He stood centimetres from Dan and me. If I wanted to, I could reach out and grab his leg.

I struggled to see his face. But it was hidden by the couch. And I didn't dare raise myself up higher.

I heard the *clonk* of wood against wood. Two dummy hands hitting each other.

I heard the rustle of heavy cloth. The *thud* of leather shoes bumping each other.

The intruder had picked up a dummy off the chair.

Squinting into the deep blackness, I could see him swing the dummy over his shoulder. I could see the dummy arms swaying, swaying at his back.

The dark figure turned away quickly. And began walking to the attic stairs.

I crept out from behind the couch. Moving on tiptoe, I began to follow the intruder.

Pressed against the wall, tiptoeing as silently as I could, I moved across the room. I held my breath. I could hear Dan close behind me.

I reached the light switch just as the intruder made it to the stairs.

My hand fumbled against the wall as I reached.

Reached . . . reached for the light switch with a trembling hand.

Yes!

I flicked on the light. And Dan and I both shrieked at the same time.

"Zane!"

My brother and I both screamed his name.

Zane's eyes bulged. His mouth opened in a high, frightened wail.

I saw his knees bend. I think he nearly crumpled to the floor.

He uttered several squeaks. Then his mouth hung open. I could see he was gasping for breath.

"Zane—we caught you!" I managed to choke out.

He had Rocky draped over his shoulder.

"What—what—?" Zane struggled to speak, but no words came out. He spluttered and started to choke. The sneering dummy bounced on his shoulder.

"Zane—we figured it out," Dan told him. "Your little tricks aren't going to work."

Our cousin was still spluttering and coughing.

"We know it's been you all along," Dan told him. He stepped over and slapped Zane hard on the back a few times.

After a few seconds, Zane stopped spluttering.

Dan picked Rocky up off Zane's shoulder and started to carry him back to his chair.

"How-how-how did you know?" Zane stammered.

"We just figured it out," I told him. "What's the big idea, anyway?"

Zane shrugged. He lowered his eyes to the floor. "You know. Just having some fun."

I glared at him. "Some fun?" I cried angrily. "You tried to get us in huge trouble. You—you could have ruined our whole summer!"

Zane shrugged again. "It was kind of my turn. You know?"

"Well, we're even now," Dan chimed in.

"Right," I agreed quickly. "We're all even now—right, Zane?"

He nodded. "Yeah. I guess." A grin spread slowly over his face. "I had you guys going, didn't I? With that stupid dummy popping up everywhere you looked."

Dan and I didn't grin back.

"You fooled us," I murmured.

"You fooled everyone," my brother added.

Zane grinned. A gleeful grin. I could see how pleased he was with himself. "I guess Dan and I deserved it," I confessed.

69

"Guess you did," Zane shot back. Would he ever stop grinning?

"So now that we're even, do we have a truce?" I demanded. "No more joking around with the dummies? No more trying to scare each other or get anyone in trouble?"

Zane bit his lower lip. He thought about it a long, long time. "Okay. Truce," he said finally.

We all shook hands solemnly. Then we slapped each other high fives. Then the three of us started laughing. I'm not sure why. The laughter just burst out of us.

Crazy giggling.

I guess because it was so late and we were so sleepy. And we were so glad we could be friends now. We didn't have to play tricks on each other any more.

As we made our way down the stairs, I felt really happy.

I thought all the scary stuff with the dummies was over.

I had no way of knowing that it was just beginning.

70

16

The next morning, Dan, Zane and I went for a long bike ride. The strong winds had faded away during the night. A soft breeze, warm and fresh-smelling, followed us as we pedalled along the path.

The trees were still winter bare. The ground glistened with a silvery morning frost. But the sweet, warm air told me that spring was on its way.

We biked slowly, following a dirt path that curved into the woods. The sun, still low in the sky, warmed our faces. I stopped to unzip my jacket. And pointed to a patch of green daffodil leaves just beginning to poke up from the ground.

"Only three more months of school!" Dan cried. He raised both fists in the air and let out a cheer.

"We're going to camp this summer for the first time," I told Zane. "Up in Massachusetts."

"For eight weeks!" Dan added happily.

Zane brushed back his blond hair. He leaned over the handlebars of my dad's bike and began pedalling harder. "I don't know what I'm doing this summer," he said. "Probably just hanging out."

"What do you *want* to do this summer?" I asked him.

He grinned at me. "Just hang out."

We all laughed. I was in a great mood and so were the guys.

Dan kept pulling wheelies, leaning way back and raising his front tyre off the ground. Zane tried to do it—and crashed into a tree.

He went sailing to the ground, and the bike fell on top of him. I expected him to whine and complain. That's his usual style. But he picked himself up, muttering, "Smooth move, Zane."

"I want to see that one again!" Dan joked.

Zane laughed. "You try it!"

He brushed the dirt off his jeans and climbed back on to the bike. We pedalled on down the path, joking and laughing.

I think we were in such great moods because of the truce. We could finally relax and not worry about who was trying to terrify who.

The dirt path ended at a small, round pond. The pond gleamed in the sunlight, still half-frozen from the long winter.

Zane climbed off his bike and rested it on the

tall grass. Then he stepped up to the edge of the pond to take photos.

"Look at the weeds poking up from the melting ice!" he exclaimed, clicking away. "Awesome. Awesome!" He knelt down low and snapped a lot of weed photos.

Dan and I exchanged glances. I couldn't see what was so special about the weeds. But I guess that's why I'm not a photographer.

As Zane stood up, a tiny brown-and-black chipmunk scampered along the edge of the pond. Zane swung his camera and clicked off a couple of shots.

"Hey! I think I got him!" he declared happily.

"Great!" I cried. Everything seemed great this morning.

We hung out at the pond for a while. We took a short walk through the woods. Then we started to get hungry for lunch. So we rode back to the house.

We were about to return the bikes to the garage when Zane spotted the old well at the back of our garden. "Cool!" he cried, his blue eyes lighting up. "Let's check it out!"

Holding his camera in one hand, he hopped off his bike and went running across the grass to the well.

It's a round, stone well with green moss covering and smooth grey stones. It used to have a pointed red roof over it. But the roof blew off during a bad storm, and Dad hauled it away.

When we were little, Dan and I used to scare each other by pretending that monsters and trolls lived down inside it. But we hadn't paid much attention to the old well in years. Dad kept saying he was going to tear it down and cover it up. But he never got round to it.

Zane clicked a lot of photos. "Is there still water down there?" he asked.

I shrugged. "I don't know."

Dan grabbed Zane around the waist. "We could throw you down and see if you make a splash!" he declared.

Zane wrestled himself out of my brother's grasp. "I've got a better idea." He picked up a stone and dropped it down the well.

After a long wait, we heard a splash far down below.

"Cool!" Zane exclaimed. He took several more pictures until he had finished the roll.

Then we made our way inside the house for lunch. We hurried upstairs to clean up.

Zane stopped at the doorway to his room.

I saw his eyes bulge and his mouth drop open. I saw his face go white.

Dan and I ran up next to him.

We stared into the bedroom—and cried out in horror.

74

"The r-room—it's been *trashed*!" Dan stammered.

The three of us huddled in the doorway, staring into the bedroom. Staring at an unbelievable mess.

At first I thought maybe Zane had left the windows open all night, and the strong winds had blown everything around.

But that didn't make any sense.

All of the clothes had been pulled out of the wardrobe and thrown over the floor. The dressing-table drawers had all been pulled out and dumped over the carpet.

The bookshelves had been emptied. Books littered the floor, the bed—they were everywhere. One bed table was turned on its side. The other stood upside down on top of the bed. A lamp lay on the floor in front of the wardrobe. Its shade was ripped and broken.

"Look—!" Zane pointed into the centre of the room.

Sitting on a tangled hill of clothes was Rocky. The dummy sat straight up, his legs crossed casually in front of him. He sneered at us as if daring us to enter.

"I-I really don't believe this!" I cried, tugging at the sides of my hair.

"*What* don't you believe?"

Mum's voice made me jump.

I turned to see her coming out of her bedroom. She tucked her blue sweater into her jeans as she walked towards us.

"Mum—!" I cried. "Something terrible has happened!"

Her smile faded. "What on earth—?" she started.

I stepped aside so she could see into Zane's room.

"Oh, no!" Mum cried out and raised both hands to her cheeks. She swallowed hard. "Did someone break in?" Her voice sounded tiny and frightened.

I peered quickly into my room across the hall. "No. I don't think so," I reported. "This is the only room that's messed up."

"But—but—" Mum spluttered. Then her eyes stopped on Rocky on top of the pile of clothes. "What is *he* doing down here?" Mum demanded.

"We don't know," I told her.

76

"But who *did* this?" Mum cried, still pressing her hands against her cheeks.

"We didn't!" Dan declared.

"We've been outside all morning," Zane added breathlessly. "It wasn't Trina, or Dan, or me. We weren't at home. We were riding bikes."

"But—someone had to do this!" Mum declared. "Someone deliberately tore this room apart."

But who was it? I wondered. My eyes darted around the mess, landing on the sneering dummy.

Who was it?

We all pitched in and helped get the room back together. It took the rest of the afternoon.

The lamp in front of the wardrobe was broken. Everything else just had to be picked up and put back where it belonged.

We worked in silence. None of us knew what to say.

At first, Mum wanted to call the police. But there was no sign that someone had broken into the house. All the other rooms were perfectly okay.

Dad returned home from the camera shop while we were still cleaning up. He, of course, was furious. "What do I have to do? Bolt the attic door?" he shouted at Dan and me.

He grabbed up Rocky and slung the dummy over his shoulder. "This isn't a joke any more," Dad said, narrowing his eyes at both of us. "This isn't funny. This is serious."

"But we didn't do it!" I protested for the hundredth time.

"Well, the dummy didn't do it," Dad shot back. "That's one thing I know for sure."

I don't know *anything* for sure, I thought. I stared at Rocky's sneering face as Dad started to walk down the hall to the attic stairs. Then I bent down to pick up the broken lamp from the floor.

That night I dreamed once again about ventriloquist's dummies.

I saw them dancing. A dozen of them. All of Dad's dummies from upstairs.

I saw them dancing in Zane's room. Dancing over the tangled piles of clothes and books. Dancing over the bed. Over the toppled bed table.

I saw Rocky dancing with Miss Lucy. I saw Wilbur doing a frantic, crazy dance on top of the dressing-table. And I saw Smiley, the new dummy, clapping his wooden hands, bobbing his head, grinning, grinning from the middle of the room as the other dummies danced around him.

They waved their big hands over their heads. Their skinny legs twisted and bent.

They danced in silence. No music. No sound at all.

And as their bodies twisted and swayed, their faces remained frozen. They grinned at one another with blank, unblinking eyes. Grinned their frightening, red-lipped grins.

Bobbed and bent, tilted and swayed, grinning, grinning, grinning the whole time in the eerie silence.

And then the grins faded as I pulled myself out of the dream.

I opened my eyes. Slowly woke up.

Felt the heavy hands on my neck.

Stared up into Rocky's ugly face.

Rocky on top of me. The dummy on top of my blanket. Over me.

Reaching. Reaching his heavy wooden hands for my throat!

I opened my mouth in a shrill scream of horror.

My hands shot out. I grabbed the dummy's hands.

I thrashed my legs. Kicked off the blanket. Kicked at the dummy.

The big eyes stared at me as if startled.

I grabbed his head. Shoved him down.

I sat up, my entire body trembling. Then I grabbed the dummy's waist.

And flung him to the floor.

The ceiling light flashed on. Mum and Dad burst into my room together.

"What's happening?"

"Trina—what's wrong?"

They both stopped short when they saw the dummy sprawled on the floor beside my bed.

"He—he—" I gasped, pointing down at Rocky. I struggled to catch my breath. "Rocky—he jumped on me. He tried to choke me. I-I woke up and—"

Dad let out a loud growl and tore at his hair. "This has got to stop!" he bellowed.

Mum dropped down beside me on the bed and wrapped me in a hug. I couldn't stop my shoulders from trembling.

"It was so scary!" I choked out. "I woke up— and there he was!"

"This is out of control!" Dad screamed, shaking his fist in the air. "Out of control!"

Mum calmed me down. Then she and I both had to calm Dad down.

Finally, after everyone was calm, they turned out the light and made their way out of the room. They closed the door. I heard Dad carrying Rocky back up to the attic.

Maybe Dad *should* get a lock for the attic door, I thought.

I shut my eyes and tried not to think about Rocky, or Zane, or the dummies—or anything at all.

After a while, I must have drifted back to sleep.

I don't know how much time passed.

I was awakened by a knock on the door. Two sharp knocks and then two more.

I sat straight up with a gasp.

I knew that Rocky had come back.

The bedroom door creaked open slowly.

I took a deep breath and held it, staring through the dark.

"Trina—?" a voice whispered. "Trina—are you awake?"

As the door opened, a rectangle of grey light spilled into the room from the hallway. Dan poked his head in, then took a few steps across the floor.

"Trina? It's me."

I let out my breath in a long *whoosh*. "Dan— what do you want?" My voice was hoarse from sleep.

"I heard everything," Dan said, stepping up beside the bed. He pulled down one pyjama sleeve. Then he raised his eyes to me. "Zane put Rocky on your bed. Zane did it!" Dan whispered.

"Huh? Why do you say that? We all have a truce—remember? Zane agreed the tricks were all over."

"Right," Dan whispered. "And now Zane thinks he can *really* scare us. Because we don't suspect him any longer. Zane hasn't given up, Trina. I'm sure of it."

I bit my lower lip. I tried to think about what Dan was saying. But I was so sleepy!

Dan leaned close and whispered excitedly. "This morning before we went biking, Zane went up to his room—remember? He said he'd forgotten his camera. So . . . he had time to mess up his room. Before he left the house."

"Yeah. Maybe," I murmured.

"And tonight he brought Rocky down and put him up on your bed. I'm sure of it," Dan insisted. "I'm sure it's Zane. We have to hide up in the attic again. Tomorrow night. We'll catch Zane again. I know we will."

"Hide up there again? No way!" I cried. "It's hot up there. And too creepy. And I'm staying as far away from those dummies as I can."

My brother sighed. "I know I'm right," he whispered.

"I don't know *what* I know," I replied. "I don't know anything about anything." I slid under the covers, pulled the blanket over my head, and tried to get back to sleep.

The next night, Mum and Dad had a dinner party in honour of Zane and Uncle Cal. They invited the Birches and the Canfields from down the street, and Cousin Robin and her husband Fred.

Fred is a great guy. Everyone calls him Froggy because he can puff out his cheeks like a frog. Froggy is short and very round and really looks like a frog.

He always makes me laugh. He knows a million great jokes. Robin is always trying to get him to shut up. But he never does.

Mum and Dad don't have many dinner parties. So they had to work all day to get the dining room ready. To set the table. And to cook the dinner.

Mum made a leg of lamb. Dad cooked up his speciality—Caribbean-style scalloped potatoes. Very spicy.

Mum bought flowers for the table. She and Dad brought out all the fancy plates and glasses that we usually see only on holidays.

The dining room really looked awesome as we all sat down to dinner. Dan, Zane and I were down at the far end of the table. Froggy sat at our end. I suppose, because he's just a big kid.

Froggy told me a moron joke. Someone asks a moron: "Can you stand on your head?" And the moron says, "No, I can't. It's up too high."

I started to laugh when I saw Zane jump up from the table. "Where are you going?" I called after him.

Zane turned back at the dining room doorway.

"To get my camera," he replied. "I want to take some pictures of the table before it gets all messed up."

He disappeared upstairs.

A few seconds later, we all heard him scream.

Chairs scraped the floor as everyone jumped up. We all went running up the stairs.

I reached Zane's room first. From the doorway, I saw him standing in the centre of the room.

I saw the sick look on Zane's face.

And then I saw the camera in his hand.

Or what was left of the camera.

It looked as if it had been run over by a truck. The film door had been twisted off and lay on the floor. The lens was smashed. The whole camera body was bent and broken.

Zane turned the camera over in his hands, gazing down at it sadly, shaking his head.

I raised my eyes to the bed. And saw Rocky sitting on the bedspread. A roll of grey film unspooled across his lap.

Dad burst into the room. All of our other guests pushed in after him.

"What happened?" someone asked.

"Is that Zane's camera?"

"What's going on?"

"That's what happens when you try to take my picture!" Froggy joked.

No one laughed. It wasn't funny.

Dad's face turned dark red as he took the camera from Zane's hand. Dad examined it carefully. His expression remained grim.

"This isn't mischief any more," he murmured. I could barely hear him over all the other voices in the room. Everyone had begun talking at once.

"This cannot be allowed," Dad said solemnly. He raised his eyes to Dan, then me. He stared at us both for the longest time without saying anything.

Zane let out a long sigh. I turned and saw that he was about to cry.

"Zane—" I started.

But he uttered an angry shout. Then he pushed past Froggy and Mr and Mrs Birch. And went running from the room.

"Someone here has done a very sick thing," Dad said sadly. He raised the camera to his face, running a finger over the broken lens. "This is a very expensive camera. It was Zane's most prized possession."

All of our guests became very quiet.

Dad kept his eyes on Dan and me. He started to say something else.

But then we all heard the deafening crash from downstairs.

21

"What is going *on* here?" Dad cried. He tossed the broken camera on to the bed and darted from the room.

The others went hurrying after him. All talking at once. I heard their shoes pounding down the stairs.

I turned to Dan. "Still think Zane is doing these things?"

Dan shrugged. "Maybe."

"No way," I told him. "No way Zane is going to smash his own camera. He loved his camera. No way he would smash it just to get you and me in trouble."

Dan raised troubled eyes to me. "Then I don't get it," he said in a tiny voice. I could see the fear on his face.

I heard startled shouts and cries of alarm from downstairs. "Let's check out the *next* disaster," I said, rolling my eyes.

We reached the bedroom door at the same

time and squeezed through together. Then I led the way along the hall and down the stairs.

I fought back my own fear as we approached the dining room.

Something very strange was going on in this house, I knew. Dad was right when he said it was no joke.

Tearing Zane's room apart wasn't a joke. It was evil.

Wrecking Zane's camera was evil, too.

Thinking about Rocky gave me a chill. The dummy was always there. Whenever something evil happened, there sat Rocky.

Trina, don't be crazy! I scolded myself. Don't start thinking that a wooden ventriloquist's dummy can be evil.

That's crazy thinking. That's really messed up. *But what could I think?*

My throat tightened. My mouth suddenly felt very dry.

I took a deep breath and led the way into the dining room.

I saw Dad in the kitchen doorway. He had his arm around Mum's shoulders. Mum had her head buried against Dad's shirtsleeve.

Was she crying?

Yes.

The guests all stood against the wall, shaking their heads, their expressions grim and confused. They muttered quietly, staring at the disaster.

The disaster. The terrible disaster.

The dining room table.

I saw the overturned platters first. Dad's scalloped potatoes smeared over the tablecloth. Clumps of potatoes stuck to the wall and the front of the china cabinet.

The salad poured over the floor and the chairs. The bread ripped into small chunks, the chunks tossed over the table. The flowers ripped off their stems. The vase on its side, water pouring over the tablecloth, puddling on the floor.

The glasses all turned over. A bottle of red wine tipped over, a dark red stain spreading over the tablecloth.

I heard Mum's sobs. I heard the sounds of Dad's muttered attempts to calm her down. I saw the other guests shaking their heads, their faces so upset, so concerned, so puzzled.

And then Dan grabbed my shoulder and pointed towards the head of the table. And I saw two dummies sitting there on dining room chairs.

Wilbur and the new dummy. Wilbur and Smiley.

They sat at the table, grinning at each other, wine glasses in their hands. As if celebrating. As if toasting each other.

That night, Dan and I hid behind the couch in the attic once again. The attic stretched dark and silent. So dark, I could barely see my brother sitting beside me.

We were both in pyjamas. The air was hot and dry. But my hands and my bare feet felt cold and clammy.

We talked softly, our legs stretched out on the floor, resting against the back of the couch. As we talked, we waited—and listened. Listened to every sound.

It was nearly midnight, but I didn't feel sleepy. I felt alert. Ready for anything.

Ready to catch Zane in the act once again.

This time, I brought my little flash camera with me. When Zane crept up here to carry one of the dummies downstairs, I'd snap his photo. Then I'd have proof to show Mum and Dad.

Yes, I'd finally decided that Dan was right.

Zane had to be the one who was destroying our house. Destroying our house and trying to scare everyone into thinking the dummies had come to life.

"But why?" I whispered to Dan. "Did we scare Zane so badly the last time he was here? So badly that he'll do *anything* to pay us back?"

"He's sick," Dan muttered. "That's the only answer. He's totally messed up."

"So messed up that he wrecked his own camera," I murmured, shaking my head.

"So messed up that he ran downstairs and trashed the dining room," Dan added.

The dining room. That's what convinced me that Zane was guilty.

All of us were upstairs in Zane's room, examining his broken camera.

Zane was the only other person downstairs.

Zane was the only person in the house who could have trashed the dining room and wrecked the dinner.

Of course he acted horrified and shocked. Of course he acted as if he didn't have a clue about what had happened.

What a sad, sad night.

The dinner guests didn't know what to say to Mum and Dad. It was such a frightening mystery. No one had an answer.

The guests helped clean up the mess. The food

was ruined. It couldn't be eaten. No one felt like eating, anyway.

Everyone left as soon as the dining room was cleaned and cleared.

As the last guest left, I turned to Dan. "Uh-oh," I whispered. "Family Conference Time. We're in for a major lecture now."

But I was wrong. Mum hurried up to her room. And Dad said he was too disgusted to talk to anyone.

Uncle Cal asked if Dad would like him to take the car and pick up some fried chicken or hamburgers or something.

Dad just scowled at him and stomped away. He carried Smiley and Wilbur up to the attic. I heard him slam the attic door. Then he disappeared into the bedroom to help comfort Mum.

Zane turned to his dad. "I-I can't believe my good camera is smashed," he whimpered.

Uncle Cal placed a hand on Zane's shoulder. "I'll bet your uncle Danny has a new camera at his shop that he'll want to give you."

"But I liked my *old* camera!" Zane wailed.

And that's when I decided he was guilty. He's a phony, I decided. He's carrying on like this— putting on a show for Dan and me.

But I wasn't going to fall for it. No way.

I made sure I had film in my little camera. Then I grabbed Dan and we crept up to the attic to wait. To wait in the darkness and catch Zane.

To end the disasters in our house once and for all.

We didn't have to wait long.

After about half an hour, I heard the tap of soft footsteps on the attic floor.

I sucked in my breath. My whole body tensed, and I nearly dropped the camera.

Beside me, Dan raised himself to his knees.

My heart pounding, I crept to the edge of the couch.

Tap tap. Shuffling footsteps on the bare floorboards.

I saw a dark figure bend down and lift a dummy off a chair.

"It's Zane," I whispered to Dan. "I knew it!"

In the heavy darkness, I could see him carrying the dummy to the stairs.

I stood up. My legs trembled. But I moved quickly.

I raised the camera. Stepped in front of the couch.

Pushed the shutter button.

The room flashed in an explosion of white light.

I clicked off another one.

Another bright white flash.

And in the flash, I saw Rocky dangling over Zane's shoulder.

No.

94

Not Zane!

Not Zane. Not Zane.

In the flash of light, I saw Rocky dangling over *another dummy's* shoulder!

Smiley! The new dummy.

The new dummy was shuffling towards the stairs, carrying Rocky away.

The dummy turned.

My hand fumbled for the light switch. I clicked on the light.

I stood frozen in front of the couch. Too startled to move.

"Smiley—stop!" I screamed.

The dummy's grin faded. The eyes narrowed at me. "I'm not Smiley," he croaked. He had a hoarse, raspy voice. "My name is Slappy."

He turned back to the stairs.

"Stop him!" I cried to my brother.

We both made a dive for the dummy.

Slappy spun around. He pulled Rocky off his shoulder—and heaved him at Dan.

I grabbed Slappy around the waist and tackled him to the floor.

He swung both hands hard. One of them slammed into my forehead.

"Unh." I let out a groan as the pain shot through me.

My hands slid off the dummy's slender waist. Slappy jumped nimbly to his feet, his grin wide and leering.

He was enjoying this!

He kicked me in the side with the toe of his big leather shoe.

My head still throbbing, I rolled out of the way. And turned back in time to see Dan grab the dummy from behind.

Dan drove his head into the dummy's back. They both dropped hard to the floor.

"Let go of me, slave!" Slappy demanded in his ugly, hoarse voice. "You are my slave now! Let go of me! I order you!"

I pulled myself to my knees as Dan and Slappy wrestled over the floor.

"He's so . . . *strong*!" Dan called out to me.

Slappy rolled on top of him. Started to pound him with his wooden fists.

I grabbed Slappy by the shoulders and tugged with all my strength. Slappy swung his arms, thrashing at my brother.

I pulled hard, trying to tug him off Dan's stomach.

"Let go! Let go!" the dummy shrieked. "Let go, slave!"

"Get off him!" I cried.

We were making such a racket, I didn't hear the attic door open downstairs. And I didn't hear the footsteps running up the stairs.

A face appeared. And then a large body.

"Dad!" I cried breathlessly. "Dad—look!"

"What on earth—!" Dad exclaimed.

"Dad—it's alive! The dummy is alive!" I shrieked.

"Huh?" Squinting through his glasses, Dad lowered his gaze to the dummy on the floor.

The dummy sprawled lifelessly on its back beside Dan. One arm was twisted beneath its back. Both legs were bent in two.

The mouth hung open in its painted grin. The eyes stared blankly at the ceiling.

"It *is* alive!" Dan insisted. "It really is!"

Dad stared down at the still, silent dummy.

"The dummy picked up Rocky!" Dan declared in a high, excited voice. "He said his name was Slappy. He picked up Rocky. He was carrying him downstairs."

Dad *tsk-tsked* and shook his head. "Give it up, Dan," he murmured angrily. "Just stop it right now." He raised his eyes to Dan, then to me. "I knew you two were the troublemakers."

"But, Dad—" I protested.

"I'm not an idiot," Dad snapped, scowling at me. "You can't expect me to believe a stupid story about a dummy coming to life and carrying another dummy around. Have you both lost your minds entirely?"

"It's true," Dan insisted.

We both gazed down at Slappy. He sure didn't

look alive. For a moment, I had the frightening feeling that I'd dreamed the whole scene.

But then I remembered something. "I have proof!" I cried. "Dad, I can prove to you that Dan and I aren't lying."

Dad rubbed the back of his neck. "I'm so tired," he moaned. "It's been such a long, horrible day. Please. Give me a break, Trina."

"But I took some pictures!" I told him. "I have pictures of Slappy carrying Rocky!"

"Trina, I'm warning you—" Dad started.

But I spun away, searching for my camera. Where was it? Where?

It took me a few seconds to spot it on the floor against the wall back by the couch. I hurried across the room to grab it.

And stopped halfway.

The back of the camera—it had sprung open. The film was exposed. The pictures were ruined.

The camera must have flown out of my hand when I tried to tackle Slappy, I realized. I picked it up and examined it sadly.

No pictures. No proof.

I turned back to find Dad scowling at me. "No more wasting my time, Trina. You two are grounded until further notice. I'm so disgusted with both of you. Your mother and I will think of other punishments after your cousin leaves."

Then Dad waved a hand at Slappy and Rocky. "Put them away. Right now. And stay out of the attic. Stay away from my dummies. That's all I have to say to you. Good night."

Dad turned away sharply and stomped down the stairs.

I glanced at Dan and shrugged. I didn't know what to say.

My heart was pounding. I was so angry. So upset. So *hurt*. My chest felt about to explode.

I bent down to pick up Slappy.

The dummy winked at me.

His ugly grin grew wider. And then he puckered his red lips and made disgusting, wet kissing sounds.

"Don't touch me, slave," Slappy growled.

I gasped and jumped back. I still couldn't believe this was happening. I wrapped my arms around myself to stop my body from trembling.

"You—you really are alive?" Dan asked softly.

"You bet your soft head I am!" the dummy roared.

"What do you want?" I cried. "Why are you doing this to us? Why are you getting us in all this trouble?"

The ugly grin spread over his face. "If you treat me nice, slaves, maybe I won't get you in any more trouble. Maybe you'll get lucky." He tapped his head and added, "Knock on wood."

"We're not your slaves!" I insisted.

He tossed back his head and let out a dry laugh. "Who's the dummy here?" he cried. "You or me?"

"You carried Rocky downstairs all those times?" Dan asked. I could see that my brother was having a hard time believing this, too.

"You don't think that bag of kindling can move on his own, do you?" Slappy sneered. "I had some fun with that ugly guy. I put him at the scene of the crimes to throw you off the track. To keep you slaves guessing."

"And you smashed Zane's camera and ruined the dinner party?" I demanded.

He narrowed his eyes to evil slits. "I'll do much worse if you slaves don't obey me."

I could feel the anger rising through my body. "You—you're going to ruin everything!" I screamed at him. "You're going to ruin our lives! You're going to keep us from going to camp this summer!"

Slappy sniggered. "You won't be going to camp. You'll be staying home to take good care of *me*!"

And then I exploded.

"Nooooo!" I uttered a long wail of protest.

I grabbed his head in both hands. I started to tug.

I remembered his head had been split in two when Dad found him. I planned to pull his head apart—to split it in two again!

He kicked his legs frantically and thrashed his arms.

His heavy shoes kicked at my legs.

But I held on tight. Pulling. Pulling. Struggling to pull his head apart.

"Let me try! Let me try!" Dan called.

I let out a sigh and dropped the dummy to the floor. "It's no use," I told Dan. "Dad did too good a job. It's glued tight."

Slappy scrambled to his feet. He shook his head. "Thanks for the head massage, slave! Now rub my back!" He laughed, an ugly dry laugh that sounded more like a cough.

Dan stared at the dummy in wide-eyed horror. "Trina—what are we going to do?" he cried, his voice just above a whisper.

"How about a game of Kick the Dummy Down the Stairs?" Slappy suggested, leering at us. "We'll take turns being the dummy. You can go first!"

"We—we have to do something!" Dan stammered. "He's a *monster*! He's evil! We have to get rid of him!"

But how? I wondered.

How?

And then I had an idea.

Slappy must have read my thoughts. He turned and started to run.

But I dived quickly—and wrapped my hands around his skinny legs.

He let out a harsh, angry cry as I began twisting his legs around each other, struggling to tie them in a knot.

He swung an arm. The wooden hand caught me on the ear.

But I held on.

"Dan—grab his arms! Hurry!"

My brother moved quickly. Slappy tried to bat him away. But Dan ducked low. And when he came up, he grabbed Slappy's wrists and held on.

"Let me go, slaves!" the dummy rasped. "Let me go now. You'll be sorry! You'll pay!"

I saw the fear on Dan's face.

Slappy swung a hand free. He tried to swipe at Dan's throat.

But Dan reached out and grabbed on to the loose arm again.

I felt eyes on me. I glanced up to see the other dummies around the room. They appeared to watch us struggle. A silent, still audience.

I pulled a red kerchief off a dummy's neck. And I stuffed it into Slappy's mouth to keep him quiet.

"Downstairs! Hurry!" I instructed my brother.

The dummy twisted and squirmed, trying to break free.

But I had his legs tied around each other. And Dan kept a tight grip on his arms.

We began making our way to the attic stairs. "Where are we taking him?" Dan demanded.

"Outside," I replied. The dummy bucked and squirmed. I nearly dropped him.

"In our pyjamas?" Dan asked.

I nodded and began backing down the stairs. Slappy struggled hard to get free. I nearly lost my balance and toppled over backwards.

"We're not going far," I groaned.

Somehow we made it all the way downstairs. I had to let go with one hand to open the front door. Slappy bucked his knees, trying to untangle his legs.

I pushed the door open. Grabbed the legs again.

Dan and I carried the squirming dummy outside.

A cold, clear night. A light, silvery frost over the grass. A half moon high over the trees.

"Ohhh." I let out a moan as my bare feet touched the frozen grass.

"It's c-cold!" Dan stammered. "I can't hold on much longer."

I saw him shiver. The front lawn suddenly darkened as clouds rolled over the moon. My legs trembled. The damp cold seeped through my thin pyjamas.

"Where are we taking him?" Dan whispered.

"Around to the back."

Slappy kicked hard. But I held on tightly.

Something scampered past my bare feet. I heard scurrying footsteps over the frosty ground.

A rabbit? A raccoon?

I didn't stop to see. Gripping Slappy's ankles with both hands, I backed up. Backed along the side of the house.

"My feet are numb!" Dan complained.

"Almost there," I replied.

Slappy uttered hoarse cries beneath the kerchief that gagged his mouth. His round eyes rolled wildly. Again, he tried to kick free.

Dan and I hauled him to the back of the garden. By the time we got to the old well, my feet were frozen numb, too. And my whole body shook from the cold.

"What are we going to do?" Dan asked in a tiny voice.

The clouds rolled away. Shadows pulled back. The silvery moonlight lit up the old stone well.

"We're going to throw him down the well," I groaned.

Dan stared at me, surprised.

"He's evil," I explained. "We have no choice."

Dan nodded.

We lifted Slappy on to the smooth stones at the top of the well. He bucked and kicked. He tried to scream through his gag.

I saw Dan shiver again.

"It's a wooden dummy," I told him. "It isn't a person. It's an evil wooden dummy."

We both shoved hard at the same time.

The dummy slid off the stone wall and dropped into the well.

Dan and I both waited until we heard the splash from far below.

Then we ran side by side back to the house.

He's gone! I thought gratefully. Joyfully. The evil thing is gone for good.

I slept really well that night. And I didn't dream about dummies.

The next morning, Dan and I met in the hall. We both were smiling. We felt so good.

I was actually singing as I followed Dan down the stairs for breakfast.

Dad greeted us at the kitchen door with an angry frown. "What is *he* doing down here?" Dad demanded.

He pointed into the kitchen.

Pointed at the breakfast table.

Pointed to Slappy, sitting at the breakfast table, grinning his ugly painted grin, his eyes wide and innocent.

Dan's mouth dropped open.

I let out a sharp cry.

"Don't act stunned. Just get him out of here," Dad said angrily. "And why is he all wet? Did you have him out in the rain?"

I glanced out of the kitchen window. Lightning flashed through a dark grey sky. Sheets of rain pounded the glass. Thunder rumbled overhead.

"Not a very nice morning," Uncle Cal said, stepping up behind Dan and me.

"I've got coffee ready," Dad told him.

"I see your friend here beat us down to breakfast," Uncle Cal said, motioning to Slappy.

The dummy's grin seemed to grow wider.

"Get him out of here, Trina," Dad repeated sharply. "Anyone want pancakes this morning?" He moved to the cabinet and started searching for a frying pan.

"Make a few extra for me. I'm starving," Uncle

Cal said. "I'll go and see if Zane is up." He turned and hurried out of the kitchen.

Dad leaned into the cabinet, banging pots and pans, searching for the one he always used for pancakes.

"Dad, I have to tell you something," I said softly. I couldn't hold it in any longer. I had to tell Dad the truth. I had to tell him the whole story.

"Dad, Slappy is evil," I told him. "He's alive, and he's evil. Dan and I threw him down the well last night. We had to get rid of him. But now—he's back. You have to help us, Dad. We have to get rid of him—now."

I took a deep breath and let it out. It felt so good to get the story off my chest.

Dad pulled his head from the cabinet and turned to me. "Did you say something, Trina? I was making such a racket, I couldn't hear you."

"Dad, I-I—" I stammered.

"Get that dummy *out* of here—now!" Dad shouted. He stuck his head back into the cabinet. "How can a whole frying pan disappear into thin air?"

I let out a disappointed sigh. A loud burst of thunder made me jump.

I motioned with my head for Dan to help me. We lifted Slappy off the chair. I held him around the waist, as far away from me as possible.

His grey suit was sopping wet. Water dripped off his black leather shoes.

We were halfway up the attic stairs when Slappy blinked and let out a soft chuckle. "Nice try, slaves," he rasped. "But give up. I'm never going away. Never!"

What a dreary morning.

Rain pounded the windows. Lightning crackled through the charcoal-grey sky. Thunder boomed so close it rocked the house.

I felt as if the storm were inside my head. As if the heavy, heavy storm clouds were weighing me down. As if the thunder erupted inside my brain, drowning out my thoughts.

Dan and I slumped on the couch in the den, watching the storm through the venetian blinds over the big window. We were trying to come up with an idea, a way to get rid of Slappy.

The room was chilly. Damp, cold air leaked through the old window. I rubbed the sleeves of my sweater, trying to warm myself.

We were alone in the house. Mum, Dad, Uncle Cal and Zane had gone into town.

"I tried to tell Dad," I said. "You heard me, Dan. I tried to tell him about Slappy. But he didn't hear me."

112

"Dad wouldn't believe you anyway, Trina," Dan replied glumly. He sighed. "Who *would* believe it?"

"How can a wooden dummy come to life?" I asked, shaking my head. "How?"

And then I remembered.

And then I had an idea.

I jumped up from the couch. I tugged my brother by the arm. "Come on."

He pulled back. "Where?"

"To the attic. I think I know how to put Slappy to sleep—for good."

I stopped at the attic door and held Dan back. "Be very quiet," I instructed him. "Maybe Slappy is asleep. If he's asleep, my plan will go a whole lot better."

Thunder roared as I opened the door. I led the way up the stairs, moving slowly, carefully, one step at a time. I could hear the rain pounding down on the roof. And I could see the flicker of lightning on the low ceiling.

I stopped as I reached the top of the stairs and turned towards the dummy collection. A flash of lightning through the window cast the shadows of their heads on the wall. As the lightning flickered, the shadows all seemed to be moving.

Dan stepped up behind me. "Here we are. Now what?" he whispered.

I raised a finger to my lips and began to tiptoe

across the floor. Thunder boomed. It sounded so much louder up here under the roof!

When Dan and I dragged Slappy up here this morning, we had tossed him down on the floor. We were too freaked and frightened to spend the time propping him up on his chair. We just wanted to dump him and get away from the attic.

I saw Slappy in the flickering white lightning. Lying on his back in the centre of the floor. The other dummies sat around him, grinning their silent grins.

I took a step closer. And then another. Moving as silently as I could.

I peered down at the evil dummy. His arms were at his sides. His legs were twisted around each other.

And his eyes were closed.

Yes!

His eyes were closed. He was asleep.

I took another few steps towards Slappy. But I felt Dan's hand on my arm, tugging me back. "Trina—what are you going to do?" he whispered.

My eyes darted to Slappy. Still asleep. Thunder roared all around. It sounded as if we were standing in the middle of it.

"Remember those weird words I read?" I whispered to my brother, keeping my eyes on the evil dummy. "Remember those weird words on that slip of paper?"

Dan thought for a moment. Then he nodded.

"Well, maybe it was those words that brought him to life," I whispered. "Maybe it's some kind of secret chant."

Dan shrugged. "Maybe." He didn't sound too hopeful.

"I saw you tuck that slip of paper back into Slappy's jacket pocket," I told my brother. "I'm going to take it out and read the words again. Maybe the same words that bring him to life will also put him back to sleep."

Of *course* it was a crazy idea.

But a dummy coming to life was crazy, too. And a dummy trying to turn you into his slave was crazy.

It was *all* crazy. So maybe my idea was just crazy enough to work.

"Good luck," my brother whispered, his eyes on the sleeping dummy on the floor.

I made my way over to Slappy.

I knelt down on my knees beside him.

I took a deep breath and held it. Then slowly, slowly, I began to reach my hand down to his jacket pocket.

I knew the slip of paper was inside that pocket. Could I pull it out without waking up Slappy?

I lowered my hand. Lowered it.

My fingers touched the top of the jacket pocket.

Still holding my breath, I began to slip two fingers inside.

"*Gotcha!*" Slappy shrieked as his hands shot up. He grabbed both of my wrists and began to squeeze.

I was so stunned, I nearly fell on top of him.

As I struggled to keep my balance, his wooden hands dug into my wrists. They tightened around me, cutting into my skin.

"Let go of me!" I screamed. I struggled to pull my arms away. But he was too strong. Too strong.

The hard fingers dug into my wrists. They squeezed harder, harder—until they cut off all circulation.

"Let go of me! Let go!" My cry came out a shrill wail.

"I give the orders, ssssslave!" Slappy hissed. "You will obey me. Obey me *for ever*! Or you will pay!"

"Let go! Let me go!" I shrieked. I tugged. I struggled to my feet. I jerked my arms up and down.

But Slappy didn't loosen his hold.

His whole body bounced in the air. Hit the floor. Bounced back up as I pulled.

But his hands gripped even harder.

I couldn't free myself. And the pain—the intense pain—shot down my arms. Down my sides. Down my whole body.

"Pick me up, sssslave!" the dummy hissed. "Pick me up and put me on my chair."

"Let go!" I cried. "You're breaking my wrists! Let go!"

The dummy uttered a cold laugh in reply.

The pain shot through my body. My legs wobbled. I dropped back to my knees.

I turned in time to see Dan dive towards us.

I thought he was going to grab the dummy's hand and try to set me free.

Instead, Dan grabbed for the jacket pocket.

Slappy let go of my wrists. But not in time.

Dan pulled the slip of paper from the pocket.

Slappy swiped at Dan's hand, trying to grab the paper away.

But Dan swung around. He unfolded the paper and raised it to his face. And then he shouted out the mysterious words that were written there:

"*Karru marri odonna loma molonu karrano.*"

Would it work?

Would it put Slappy back to sleep?

I rubbed my aching wrists and stared down at the grinning dummy.

He gazed back at me. And then winked.

His laughter roared over the thunder, over the hard, steady drumming of rain on the roof.

"You cannot defeat me that way, slave!" Slappy cried gleefully.

I took a step back. A chill ran down my back, making my whole body shudder.

My plan hadn't worked.

My only plan. My last, desperate plan. A total failure.

I caught the disappointment on Dan's face. The slip of paper fell from his fingers and floated to the floor.

"You will pay for this!" Slappy threatened. "You will pay for your foolish attempt to defeat me."

He pushed his hands against the floor and started to climb to his feet.

I backed up.

And saw the other dummies move.

All of them. They were sliding off their chairs. Lowering themselves from the couch.

They stretched their skinny arms. Flexed their big, wooden hands.

Their heads bobbed, their knees bent as they started to shuffle towards us.

They had all come to life! Twelve dummies, brought to life by those strange words Dan had cried out.

Twelve dummies staggering towards Dan and me.

We were trapped between them. Trapped in the circle as they shuffled, dragging their heavy shoes. Their eyes wide. Locked on Dan and me.

As they staggered and shuffled. Moving stiffly, grinning, grinning so coldly.

Closing in on Dan and me.

Wilbur limped towards us, his big, chipped hands stretched out, ready to grab us. Lucy's big blue eyes gleamed coldly as she staggered towards us. Arnie let out a high-pitched giggle as he pulled himself closer.

Closer.

Dan and I spun around. But we had nowhere to turn. Nowhere to escape.

The dummies' big shoes scraped heavily over the wooden floorboards. Their knees bent with each step. They looked as if they would tumble to the floor.

But they kept coming. Lurching forward. Bodies bending. Heads bobbing.

Alive. Wooden creatures. Alive!

Dan raised his hands over his face as if to shield himself.

I took a step back. But the dummies behind me were closing in, too.

I took a long, deep breath and held it.

Then I waited.

Waited for their wooden hands to grab us.

I uttered a loud gasp as Wilbur and Arnie staggered right past me.

The dummies all brushed past Dan and me.

As if we weren't there.

I stared in shock as they circled Slappy. I saw Rocky grab Slappy by the collar. I saw Lucy grab Slappy's shoes.

Then the circle of dummies moved in closer. Tighter.

I couldn't see what they were doing to Slappy. But I saw their skinny arms jerking and tugging. I saw them all struggling together.

Wrestling with him.

Were they pulling him apart?

I couldn't see. But I heard Slappy's scream of terror.

Dan and I clung to each other, watching the strange sight. It looked like a rugby tackle. A tackle of dummies.

The dummies grunted and groaned, muttering in low tones as they worked over Slappy.

We couldn't see Slappy in the middle.

We heard only one scream.

We didn't hear him scream again.

And then I heard the attic door open.

Footsteps on the stairs!

Someone was coming up.

I poked Dan and turned him to the stairs.

We both cried out as Zane climbed up to the attic and squinted across the long room at us.

Did he see the struggling dummies? Did he see that they were all alive?

I turned back—in time to see the dummies all collapse in a heap.

"Whoa!" I cried, my heart pounding. I blinked several times. I didn't believe what I was seeing.

The twelve dummies lay lifeless on the floor, arms and legs in a wild tangle. Mouths open. Eyes gazing up blankly at the low ceiling.

Slappy lay sprawled in the middle. His head tilted to one side. I saw the blank stare in his eyes. Saw the open-mouthed, wooden grin.

He was completely lifeless now. As lifeless as all the others.

Had the other dummies somehow destroyed his evil?

Would Slappy remain a lifeless block of wood for ever?

I didn't have time to think about it. Zane came hurrying across the attic, an angry scowl on his face. His eyes were on the pile of dummies.

"Caught you!" Zane cried to Dan and me. "Caught you both! Planning your next trick! I *knew* you two were the ones! I'm telling Uncle Danny what you're doing!"

Of course no one believed Dan and me.

Of course everyone believed Zane.

We were in the worst trouble of our lives. Dan and I were grounded for ever. We probably won't be allowed to leave the house until we are in our forties!

The next day, Zane and Uncle Cal were at the front door, saying goodbye. It's a terrible thing to say—but Dan and I were *not* sad to see Zane go.

"I hope I never have to come back here," he whispered to me in the hall. Then he put on a big, phony smile for Mum and Dad.

"Zane, what kind of camera would you like?" Dad asked, putting a hand on Zane's shoulder. "You have a birthday coming up. I'd like to send you a new camera for your birthday."

Zane shrugged his big shoulders. "Thanks," he told my Dad. "But I'm really not into photography any more."

Mum and Dad raised their eyebrows in surprise.

"Well, what *would* you like for your birthday, Zane?" Mum asked. "Is there something else you're interested in?"

Zane shyly lowered his eyes to the floor. "Well . . . I'd kind of like to try being a ventriloquist— like you, Uncle Danny."

Dad beamed happily.

That creep Zane had said just the right thing.

"Maybe you have a spare dummy you can lend Zane," Uncle Cal suggested.

Dad rubbed his chin. "Well . . . maybe I do." He turned to me. "Trina, run up to the attic. And pick out a good dummy for Zane to take home. Not one of the old ones. But a nice one that Zane can enjoy."

"No problem, Dad," I replied eagerly. I hurried up to the attic. I hoped they didn't see the enormous grin on my face.

Can you guess which dummy I picked out for Zane?

I know it's horribly mean. But I really had no choice—did I?

"Here's a good one, Zane," I said a few seconds later. I placed the grinning dummy in Zane's arms. "His name is Slappy. I think you two will be very happy together."

I hope Zane has fun learning to be a ventriloquist.

But I have the feeling he may have a few problems. Because as Zane carried Slappy into the car, I saw the dummy wink at me.

Goosebumps

Bad Hare Day

"Pick a card, any card." I spread out the deck of cards in front of Sue Mailer, face down. She giggled and picked one.

"Don't show it to me," I warned her. She glanced at the card, keeping it hidden from me.

A small crowd of kids gathered on the school steps to watch. School was out for the day. Sue showed them her card.

I love doing magic tricks—especially in front of an audience. My dream is to be a great magician like my idol, Amaz-O.

I've been playing around with stage names. My real name is Tim Swanson—but that's far too boring for a professional magician. I've been thinking of calling myself Swanz-O. My best friend, Foz, thinks Swanz-O sounds like a washing powder.

"Now, Sue," I said in a louder voice, so everybody could hear me. "Put the card back in the deck."

Sue slipped the card in with the others. I shuffled the deck and tapped it three times. "I will now make your card rise to the top of the deck," I announced.

Tap, tap, tap. I picked up the top card and showed it to Sue. "Was this your card?" I asked her.

Her eyebrows shot up in amazement. "The three of clubs!" she cried. "That was my card!"

"How'd you do that?" Jesse Brown asked.

"Magicians never reveal their secrets," I said, bowing. "And now, for my next trick—"

"I know how he did it." My little sister, Ginny, suddenly popped up in the crowd. The sound of her scratchy voice made my hair stand on end. She loves to spoil my magic shows.

But a true magician doesn't let anything throw him. I grinned my biggest, fakest grin at the little brat.

"Ladies and gentlemen, my lovely assistant, Ginny!"

"I'm not your assistant, freak-face," Ginny snarled. "You won't catch me doing nerdy magic tricks. I'm into karate. Hi-ya!" She demonstrated her karate chop.

Some of the kids laughed. I pretended to laugh, too. "Ha, ha. Isn't she a riot?"

Everybody says Ginny looks like an angel. She has long, wavy blonde hair, rosy cheeks and big blue eyes. People always ooh and aah over her.

No one ever oohs and aahs over me. I've got curly light-brown hair and hazel eyes. I'm twelve, which Mum says isn't a "cute age".

My nose is long and curves up at the end like a hot dog. Ginny likes to flick the end of my nose with her finger and say, "Boi-oi-oing."

Her nose is small and perfect, of course.

I tried to continue my show, Ginny or no Ginny. I slipped the deck of cards into my pocket and yanked out my magic scarf. "Now, be amazed as I—"

Ginny reached into my pocket and snatched out the cards. "Look, everybody!" she cried, showing them the cards. "*All* the cards are the three of clubs!"

Ginny started passing the cards around so everyone could see.

"Hey! Give those back!" I protested. I grabbed the cards away. It was true. Every single card in the deck was the three of clubs. But no one was supposed to know that.

"You're a phony," Sue mumbled.

"No—wait!" I cried. "Watch this!"

I whipped out my magic rings—two large silver hoops hooked together. The kids quietened down a little.

"These silver rings are locked together," I declared. "They're completely solid—linked together for ever!" I tugged on them to show that they wouldn't come apart.

131

Then I handed them to Jesse. "Try to pull the rings apart," I told him. He pulled hard. He pulled lightly. He pulled hard again. He jangled them around. The rings stayed hooked together.

I took them back. "The rings will never come apart," I said. "Unless I say the magic words." I waved one hand over the rings. "Hocus pocus!" I gently pulled the rings apart. A couple of kids clapped.

"You're not going to fall for *that* old trick, are you?" Ginny mocked. "You want to know how he does it?" She grabbed the rings away and began to demonstrate. "They're trick rings—"

"I will now make my lovely assistant disappear!" I cried, shoving Ginny aside. "Beat it!"

"Stop pushing me!" she shouted. "Hi-ya!"

She karate-kicked me in the stomach.

"Oof!" I doubled over. Everybody laughed and clapped.

"That's a great trick!" Sue said.

I clutched my stomach. Some trick.

Stupid Ginny and her karate kicks. Why did Mum have to take her to that martial-arts school? My life has been miserable ever since. She's only ten, and she fights far better than I do. I've got the bruises to show it.

"Kick him again!" somebody yelled.

Ginny crouched, ready to attack.

"Try it, and I'll tell Mum where that dent in the refrigerator door came from," I warned her.

"Or that spinning box Amaz-O has," I added. Amaz-O was my hero—the greatest magician ever. "Did you see him on TV last week? His assistant stepped into a big black box. Amaz-O spun it around three times, and she disappeared!"

"He's doing a show at Midnight Mansion," Foz said. Midnight Mansion is a club in town where magicians perform every night.

"I know. I wish I could go. But the tickets cost twenty-five dollars."

We turned on to Bank Street and headed towards the centre of town. It wasn't on the way home, but Foz knew what I was doing. Malik's Magic Shoppe was on Bank Street. I stopped in there at least once a week, just to drool over the cool tricks they had.

"Malik's has a bunch of new tricks," I told Foz. "Designed by Amaz-O himself."

"I'll bet they're expensive," Foz said.

"They are." I reached into my pocket to see how much money I had. Five bucks.

"That'll buy you a squirting flower," Foz said. "Maybe."

I stuffed the bill back into my pocket. "You've got to see this stuff, anyway. There's a table— you put a plate or something on it—it can be anything you want. The plate will rise up over the table and float!"

"How does it work?" Foz asked.

135

"I don't know. Mr Malik wouldn't tell me. He said you have to buy the trick to find out."

"How much does it cost?"

"Five hundred dollars."

Foz rolled his eyes. "I guess you'll have to stick with card tricks."

"I guess." I sighed.

A little bell rang as we opened the door to Malik's. I breathed in the musty smell of the shop. It was jam-packed with old tricks, new tricks, magic books and costumes. There were even cages in the back for rabbits and doves. Mr Malik sold everything.

I called out, "Hi, Mr Malik." He stood behind the till. He was a short, bald old man with a fat stomach.

I waited for Mr Malik to say, "What's new, Magoo?" in his gravelly voice. That's how he greets all his regular customers.

I called out, "Hi!" again, but he didn't answer. He just stood there and grunted.

"Mr Malik?" Foz and I crept closer to the counter.

"Unh!" Mr Malik grunted. He stumbled forward.

Something was sticking out of his stomach. A sword!

"Mr Malik?" I asked. "Are you okay?"

He clutched the handle of the sword and moaned in pain.

Someone had stabbed him!

"Help me!" he groaned. "Please—help!"

Foz and I froze in fear. I let out a gasp—but I was too frightened to move. Foz's whole body trembled.

Mr Malik uttered another groan. Then his expression changed. He pulled out the sword—and he tossed it to me.

"Hey!" I cried. "It's a fake!"

Mr Malik laughed. He rubbed his round stomach, which hadn't been stabbed at all. "What's new, Magoo?" he chuckled. "Get a load of that trick sword. Just got it in today."

I tested the sword against my own stomach. It had a sliding blade. I pushed the blade into the handle, then let go. It popped out again. Very cool.

Foz fingered the blade. "Think of the tricks you could play on Ginny with a sword like this!"

"Like it, Tim?" Mr Malik asked. "Only twenty bucks."

I shook my head. "We're just looking, Mr Malik."

He hung the sword on the wall behind him. "All right. Take your time and look around. But would it kill you to actually *buy* something once in a while?"

Mr Malik always said that, too.

I wandered to the back of the shop. I checked out a rack of magician's jackets. I pulled a sparkly blue dinner-jacket off the rack and tried it on. It had a trick sleeve for hiding things.

I stared at myself in the mirror. I pretended to announce myself. "The Amazing Swanz-O!"

Foz shook his head in disgust. "That name is so lame."

"Yeah, you're right." I thought of another name. "How about 'Swanson the Magnificent'?"

"It's okay," Foz said. "A little boring, but okay."

He tried on a top hat and added, "You need something cooler, like 'Tim the Destroyer'."

"That sounds like a wrestler," I commented.

"At least it's not wimpy," Foz retorted. "Like Swanz-O."

"Hey, boys." Mr Malik shuffled towards us. He held out two tickets.

"Take these, if you want them," he said. "Two free passes to Amaz-O's magic show tomorrow night."

"Wow!" I cried. I took a ticket and read it.

ADMIT ONE
AN EVENING OF MAGIC WITH THE
GREAT AMAZ-O
MARCH 23
10 P.M.
MIDNIGHT MANSION

"Thanks Mr Malik! I can't believe we'll get to see Amaz-O in person!" I gushed. "Tomorrow night!"

"Tomorrow night?" Foz frowned at his ticket. "I can't go. My aunt and uncle are coming over. It's my mother's birthday."

"So? This is a once-in-a-lifetime chance! Your mother has a birthday every year."

Foz stuffed the ticket into my palm, shaking his head. "I know my mum—and she won't see it that way. Anyway, tomorrow night is a school night."

I'd forgotten about that. I hoped my mum would let *me* go. Ten o'clock was pretty late to go out on a school night.

She has to let me go, I decided. She just *has* to. What kind of horrible mother would keep her son from seeing his hero in person? Only a really mean, monstery mother.

My mother is a grump, but she's not a monster.

I took off the blue jacket and hung it back up on the rack. A large wooden box caught my eye. It was the size of a coffin, brightly painted with red and yellow stars. I lifted the lid.

The box was empty, lined with blue velvet on the inside. "What's the box do, Mr Malik?" I asked.

"That's for sawing people in half," Mr Malik replied.

I examined the inside of the box, trying to figure out how it worked. I found no secret compartments or panels or anything.

"How does it work?" I asked Mr Malik.

"You going to buy it?" he demanded.

"Well—how much does it cost?"

"Two-fifty."

"Two dollars and fifty cents? I can afford that."

Mr Malik waved me away and started towards the stockroom at the back of the shop. "Two dollars and fifty cents," he muttered. "In your dreams."

"He meant two *hundred* and fifty dollars, Brainz-O," Foz said.

I tried to cover myself. "I knew that. I was joking."

Foz fiddled with a cool-looking trick in the corner. I moved closer to see.

"It's a guillotine," Foz said. "For chopping off heads."

The guillotine had a place for the victim to rest his head at the bottom—and a razor-sharp blade at the top.

Mr Malik emerged from the back room. "I'm closing up soon, boys," he called.

"I just want to see how this works," Foz said. He twisted a lever on the guillotine.

"Foz—no!" I cried.

The blade slid down the guillotine.

And landed with a horrifying *thunk*.

"My hand!" Foz shrieked. "My hand!"

Mr Malik gasped. "I'll call an ambulance!" He grabbed the phone.

The guillotine blade had sliced right through Foz's hand. He screamed in pain.

"Oh!" Foz moaned. "I cut off my hand!" he wailed. "I'll never write again!"

I started laughing.

"Why are you laughing?" Mr Malik demanded. "This is an emergency!"

"No, it's not." Foz held up his hands to show that he was fine. "Got a paper towel? I need to wipe off this fake blood."

"Fake?" Mr Malik stammered. "Fake blood?"

"We got you back for that sword trick," I told him.

Mr Malik clutched his sweaty forehead in his hands. "I'm so stupid! I know that's a trick guillotine. Why did I fall for such a dumb joke?"

"Hey," Foz protested. "It was a lot funnier than your sword-in-the-stomach joke."

Mr Malik wiped his brow and smiled. "All right, boys. Enough tricks. It's five o'clock. Get out of here." He shoved us towards the door.

"Thanks for the tickets, Mr Malik," I called. "See you next week."

"Sure. Next week, when I'll have a new shipment of magic tricks you won't buy."

The bell on the door jangled as we left the shop. Foz and I walked down Bank Street towards home.

"Sure you won't go to Midnight Mansion tomorrow night?" I asked him.

"I can't. Your mum will never let you go, either."

"I'll find a way," I insisted. "You'll see."

We paused in front of Foz's house. "Come over to my house after school tomorrow," I said. "I'm giving another magic show. Only this time Ginny won't wreck it."

"I'll be there," Foz promised.

"And bring your sister's rabbit," I added.

Foz shuffled his feet uncomfortably. "Clare is not going to like that . . ." he began.

"Please, Foz," I begged. "I'm going to finish building my rabbit table tonight. The rabbit trick is going to be so amazing—"

"I'll try to bring the rabbit," Foz said. "But if anything happens to it, Clare will kill me."

"Nothing will happen to it—I promise."

I waved goodbye to Foz and went home. "The

Great Swanzini is here!" I announced as I burst into the kitchen.

"You mean the Great Jerk," Ginny mumbled. She sat at the kitchen table, folding napkins. She reached up and flicked at my nose. "Boi-oi-oing."

"Get off me." I slapped her hand away.

Mum set a plate of chicken on the table. "Go and wash, Tim," she ordered. "And tell your father supper is ready."

"Look, Mum." I held up a quarter. Then, with a flick of my wrist, I slipped it up my sleeve. "I made the quarter disappear!"

I showed her my two empty hands.

"Very nice. I see two hands that haven't been washed yet," Mum said impatiently.

"I saw the quarter go up your sleeve," Ginny sneered.

"No one appreciates me around here," I complained. "Someday I'm going to be the greatest magician in the world. And my own family doesn't care!"

Mum strode to the kitchen door. "Bill!" she called upstairs to my dad. "Supper!"

I made my way out of the kitchen to wash my hands. My parents didn't take my magic act seriously. They thought it was just a hobby.

But Ginny's karate lessons were the most important thing in the world, of course. Mum always said, "Girls need to know how to defend themselves." Now I needed to defend myself against my own sister!

I returned to the kitchen and sat down. Mum plunked a piece of chicken down beside the rice on my plate. Dad and Ginny were already eating.

"I had a terrible day at work today," Mum grumbled, ripping into her chicken. She's a high school guidance counsellor. "First Michael Lamb threatened to beat up another boy. His teacher yelled at him, and he threatened to beat her up, too. She sent him to my office. When I tried to talk to him, he said he'd beat *me* up. So I called his mother in—and *she* tried to beat me up. I had to call the police!"

"That's a piece of cake next to *my* day," Dad complained. Dad sells cars. "Some guy came in and said he wanted to test-drive the new minivan. I handed him the keys, and he took off. He never came back. He stole the car!"

I sighed and shovelled rice into my mouth. Dinner is like this every night. Both of my parents hate their jobs.

"I had a really tough day, too," Ginny put in. "Michael Franklin teased me. So I had to karate-kick him in the leg!"

I smirked. "Poor you."

Mum's forehead wrinkled—her concerned look. "You didn't hurt yourself, did you, Ginny?"

"No," Ginny replied. "But I *could* have."

"What about me?" I protested. "*I'm* the one who got kicked in the stomach. And it hurt a lot!"

"You seem to be fine now," Dad chimed in.

I gave up. I knew that arguing would get me nowhere. Mum and Dad always take Ginny's side.

"Is there any dessert?" Ginny demanded.

"Ice-cream," Mum answered.

"I'll clear the table," I offered, hoping it would put Mum in a better mood. I needed both Mum and Dad to be in a good mood.

Because I was about to ask the big question.

Would they let me go to Midnight Mansion tomorrow night?

Would they?

I stood up, collecting dirty plates. "Guess what? Amaz-O is doing his act at Midnight Mansion tomorrow night. Mr Malik gave me two free passes." I held my breath, waiting for their answer.

"Excellent!" Ginny cried. "That means I can go too!"

"I'm not taking you," I told her. "I'll ask Mark or Jesse or somebody. Anybody but you." I dropped the plates in the sink. They crashed but didn't break.

"Careful, Tim," Mum warned.

Ginny slithered over to the sink and tried to hug me. "Please, Tim. I'm your sister. Your only sister in the whole world. I'd do *anything* for you. You have to take me with you!"

"Neither one of you is going," Dad said quietly. "It's a school night."

"But Dad, it's free!" I protested. "Just this once. Amaz-O is my hero. I'll never get another chance to see him in person!"

"What time does the show start?" Mum asked.

"Ten o'clock," I told her.

She shook her head. "Absolutely not. You're not going out at ten o'clock on a school night. Especially not to a nightclub. You're much too young." She furiously spooned ice-cream into a bowl.

"Mum—please!" I begged. "I'm twelve. I can handle it."

"You heard your mother," Dad said. "You'll have other chances to see Amaz-O, Tim. Don't worry."

Mum offered me a bowl of ice-cream. "I don't want it," I grumbled. I stormed out of the kitchen. As I left, I heard Ginny say, "Good. Now I'll get two bowls of ice-cream."

Stupid Ginny, I thought. Stupid Mum and stupid Dad. My one chance to see my idol, the great Amaz-O—and they won't let me go.

I wandered into the garage. In the corner stood a new trick I was building—the rabbit table. It was a square table that came up to my waist. The top had a hole in it that led to a secret compartment under the table.

I planned to hide a rabbit in the compartment and cover the hole with my magic top hat. When I pressed a pedal at the foot of the table, the bottom of the secret compartment would rise up. Then I'd lift my hat—and there would be the rabbit!

The table was almost finished. I turned it upside down and hammered on the bottom of the secret compartment.

This trick is going to knock everybody out tomorrow afternoon, I thought. I'll be almost as amazing as Amaz-O!

I was so busy hammering I didn't hear the garage door open. Two baby blue high-tops suddenly appeared in front of me. I didn't have to look up. I knew Ginny's smelly trainers when I saw them.

"Go away," I commanded.

She never listens to me. "You going to do the rabbit trick tomorrow?" she asked.

"Uh-huh. Now go away."

"Where are you going to get the rabbit?"

I set down my hammer. "I'm going to turn *you* into a rabbit."

"Ha ha." She flipped her wavy blonde hair. "You know what this table would be perfect for?" she asked. "Karate-chopping. I'll bet I could chop it in half with one hand."

"Try it and I'll—"

"You'll what?" she taunted.

What could I do to her? Not much. "I'll turn you into a rabbit for *real*," I threatened.

"Oh, yeah? How are you going to do that?"

"It's easy," I replied. "Mr Malik showed me how. Tonight, while you're sleeping, I'm going to sneak into your room and turn you into a rabbit."

148

"Give me a break," Ginny said. "That is so dumb."

"Maybe. Maybe not. I guess we'll find out tonight." I picked up my hammer again. "I hope you like carrots," I told her.

"You're crazy," she said. She hurried out of the garage.

Well, I thought. At least that got rid of her for a while.

I set the table on its legs again. All I had to do was paint it, and it would be ready.

Wouldn't it be great? I thought as I opened a can of blue paint. Wouldn't it be great if I really *could* turn Ginny into a rabbit?

But that was impossible. Wasn't it?

"We want the rabbit trick! We want the rabbit trick!"

Ginny sat in the grass in our back garden. Six or seven other kids sat around. I was in the middle of my magic act. Ginny was stirring up trouble.

She knew I didn't have a rabbit for the trick. I was still waiting for Foz to show up.

Where is he? I wondered. He's ruining my show!

The other kids joined in Ginny's chant. "The rabbit trick! The rabbit trick!"

I tried to stall them. "The amazing, incredible rabbit trick is coming up," I promised. "But first—wouldn't you like to see me pull a quarter out of Ginny's ear again?"

"No!" the kids yelled. "Boo!"

"Karate fight!" Sue called. "We want a karate fight. Ginny versus Tim!"

Things were getting ugly.

At last I glimpsed Foz at the side of the house. He waved at me frantically.

"Intermission!" I announced. "I'll be back in two minutes. And then—I'll pull a rabbit out of my hat!"

I hurried over to Foz. A big cardboard box sat at his feet.

"What took you so long?" I demanded.

"I'm sorry," Foz said. "I almost had to rip the rabbit out of Clare's hands."

I opened the box. Clare's big white rabbit lifted its nose and sniffed at me. I grabbed it and stuffed it under my jacket.

"Be careful!" Foz warned. "If anything happens to it, my sister will chop me into rabbit food!"

"The rabbit will be fine," I told him. "What could happen to it?"

I sneaked the rabbit to the table. With my back to the audience, I stuffed it into the secret compartment and plopped my hat on top.

Then I turned to face the kids. None of them had seen the rabbit. Perfect.

"Ladies and gentlemen!" I called. "Thanks for being so patient. Here is the moment you've all been waiting for—"

"Karate fight!" Ginny called.

"Even better than a karate fight!" I said. "I, the Great Timothini, will now pull a rabbit out of my hat!"

Ginny snorted. "The Great Timothini?"

I pointed at her. "You, in the front row. Quiet!"

"You be quiet!" Ginny shot back.

"Get on with it!" Jesse called.

"Okay. I need complete silence now. I must concentrate."

To my surprise, the kids actually quietened down. Even Ginny. Everyone stared up at me, waiting.

I lifted my hat off the table. "As you can see, my hat is empty. It's an ordinary, everyday top hat. Sue, will you please examine the hat?"

I passed the hat to Sue. She turned it over. "It looks like a regular hat to me," she declared.

I set the hat on the table, covering the secret compartment. "Thank you, Sue. Now—watch carefully."

I waved my arms over the hat. "Abracadabra, abracadeer, rabbit, rabbit, rabbit—*appear*!"

I stepped on the pedal to make the rabbit rise up. Then I lifted the hat with a flourish.

Nothing there. The hat stood empty.

I checked the secret compartment. No rabbit there, either.

My heart pounded. How could this be?

"The rabbit!" I cried. "It's gone!"

What have I done? I thought in horror.

My trick must have worked better than I thought!

I glanced up and saw Ginny pointing across the back garden. "There it goes!" she cried. "There's the rabbit!"

I whirled around. Clare's white rabbit was hopping away.

How could that happen? I wondered. I glanced into the secret compartment again.

I'd left one side of the secret compartment open. How could I have been so stupid?

"Tim—you promised!" Foz screamed. "Grab it!"

I chased after the rabbit. Foz huffed behind me. The rabbit had already hopped halfway across our next-door neighbours' garden. I glanced back. Ginny and the other kids were yelling and running after us.

The rabbit stopped behind a bush. I sped up— and pounced.

"Got him!" I cried. But the rabbit slipped out of my hands and bounded away.

"He's heading for the stream!" Ginny shouted.

A muddy stream ran behind all the back gardens on our block. The rabbit disappeared behind the trees that hid the stream.

Whooping like crazy, Ginny led the kids after the rabbit.

"Stop!" I yelled. "You're scaring it away!"

But none of them listened to me. There was nothing to do but keep chasing.

"Don't let the rabbit hop into the water!" Foz screamed. "He'll drown!"

"He won't drown," I told Foz. "That stream is only about five centimetres deep."

"Just catch the rabbit!" Foz ordered. He was in a total panic. Maybe his sister really *would* chop him into rabbit food.

The rabbit hopped through the mud and across the stream into the Darbys' garden. I shoved the other kids aside. I splashed through the stream.

The rabbit stopped. Its ears twitched.

I motioned to the others to keep still. I squatted down and crept towards the rabbit.

I saw why it had stopped. The Darbys' cat, Boo Boo, crouched low in the grass, waiting to pounce.

The rabbit was trapped between us. I crawled closer. Closer. I was almost there. . .

"Watch out for the cat!" Foz shrieked.

With a yowl, the cat leaped. The rabbit bounced about thirty centimetres in the air. I missed him.

Everybody raced after him again. I threw Foz a dirty look.

"You're ruining everything!" I shouted.

"*You're* the one who lost him in the first place!" Foz yelled back.

"Hey!" Sue called. "Look at Ginny!"

Ginny had raced to the head of the pack. The rabbit paused, then started running again. Ginny took a flying leap. "*Yaw, hee ha how!*" she screeched in her weirdo karate voice.

She landed on her feet in front of the rabbit. It tried to change course. Too late.

"Hiii—ya!" Ginny swooped down and grabbed the rabbit. She held him over her head like a trophy.

"I got him!" she cried. "I got him!"

"Yay, Ginny!" Everyone crowded around her, slapping her on the back.

"Don't let him go!" Foz cried. He hurried over to Ginny and snatched the rabbit away.

We all started back to my garden. "Awesome trick, Tim." Jesse patted me on the back. "You almost made the rabbit really disappear!"

Everybody laughed. "You should change your stage name, Timothini," Sue chimed in. "How about 'The Great Goofballini'?"

"Or 'Mess-Up the Magnificent'!" Jesse suggested.

I sighed and shut my eyes. Another magic show—another disaster.

"I can't believe you almost lost my sister's rabbit," Foz grumbled.

"I'm sorry, Foz. I'll be more careful next time."

He clutched the rabbit tightly to his chest. "Next time, get your own rabbit."

He hurried to the side of the house and stuffed the rabbit into the box.

"Anybody want to come over to my house?" Jesse called. He lived next door. "I've got a great trick to show you—the disappearing dog. I let go of his leash, and he runs away!"

Laughing, the other kids drifted over to Jesse's house. Foz took the rabbit home to his sister.

"You going over to Jesse's?" Ginny asked.

I shook my head. "I'm going inside for a snack."

"Maybe you should do your magic act inside from now on," Ginny said. "Then your tricks won't be able to escape from you!" She giggled.

"Very funny," I mumbled. "You won't be laughing so hard when I turn *you* into a rabbit. I don't think rabbits know how to laugh."

"Ooh. I'm scared." She rolled her eyes.

"You'd better be." I leaned close to her and whispered. "Tonight's the night. Tonight, while

156

you're sleeping, I'll turn you into a rabbit. And if you try to run away, the Darbys' cat will get you."

She rolled her eyes again. Then she reached up to tweak my nose. "Boi-oi-oing."

She trotted off to Jesse's house.

I definitely need better magic tricks, I thought as I dragged myself into the house. Better equipment, too. So I can do really *cool* tricks. Tricks that actually work.

I thought of all the stuff Mr Malik sold in his shop. If I could have just one of those tricks, I could do a great act. I've got to get one somehow.

But how?

That night everybody went to bed early. Mum and Dad were exhausted and crabby after another bad day at work.

"Today was the worst day ever!" Mum grumbled. "I'm so exhausted. Everybody to bed!"

Ginny and I knew better than to protest. We didn't want to stay up, anyway, with Mum and Dad grouching around all evening.

I lay in bed with the lights off, trying to sleep. Amaz-O's show is tonight, I thought miserably. He's performing tonight, only a few miles away from my house. I have free passes. And I can't go. It's not fair!

How am I ever going to be a great magician if I never see any magic shows? Amaz-O is the greatest of the great—and I have to miss my one chance to see him!

Or do I? A wicked thought popped into my head. Why *should* I miss the show?

I've got the tickets. I can ride to Midnight Mansion on my bike. I could sneak out of the house for a couple of hours—and Mum and Dad would never have to know.

I rolled over in bed and peered at my alarm clock. The dial glowed in the dark. Nine-forty.

The show would start in twenty minutes, I knew. I could still make it if I left right now.

I couldn't stand to think about it any longer. I had to go.

I slid out of bed, hoping my mattress wouldn't creak. I tiptoed across the room to my dressing-table. I silently pulled on a pair of jeans and a shirt.

Trainers in hand, I carefully opened my bedroom door. The house was dark. I heard Dad snoring in my parents' room down the hall.

I crept towards the stairs. Am I really doing this? I thought, suddenly nervous. Am I really sneaking out in the middle of the night to go to Midnight Mansion?

Yes—I'm really doing it, I thought. I'll do *anything* to see Amaz-O. It's totally worth the risk.

What's the worst that could happen?

Mum and Dad could find out. Then what? Maybe they'd ground me. But I will have seen the great Amaz-O in person. And while I'm grounded, I can try to learn some of Amaz-O's tricks.

Anyway, I won't get caught. I won't.

I paused at the top of the stairs. The stairs in my house are the creakiest stairs in the universe.

Once when I was little, I tried to sneak downstairs on Christmas Eve to see what Santa had left me. I barely touched the top step with my foot—*CRRREEEEAAAK!* Mum burst out of her room before I even had a chance to try the second step.

It's not going to happen this time, I told myself. I'll take each step very slowly. I'll lean on the banister to keep them from creaking. No one will wake up. No one will hear me.

I put both my hands on the banister and rested my weight on it. Then I set my right foot carefully—the toe, then the heel—on the top step.

Crick. Just a tiny little sound. I'm sure no one heard it, I thought.

I shifted my hands down the banister and took another step. This one made no creak at all.

So far, so good.

I took a third step. *Creak.* Not a rip-roaring loud creak, but louder than the first. I froze.

I listened for the sound of someone stirring in the house.

Silence. All clear.

If Amaz-O only knew what I'm going through to see him, I thought. I must be his biggest fan on the face of the earth.

I made it all the way down the stairs with only one more creak. I breathed a sigh of relief.

I'm safe now, I thought. I'll wait until I get outside to put my shoes on. Then I'll grab my bike and go.

I tiptoed across the cold hallway floor. I reached for the handle of the front door. Twisted it.

Almost there.

Almost.

Then a shrill voice demanded, "Tim—where do you think you're going?"

I spun around. Ginny!

She was dressed in jeans and a sweater, all ready to go out. She bounded down the stairs.

"Ssshhhhhhhh! You'll wake up Mum and Dad!"

I grabbed her by the arm and yanked her out of the front door.

"What are you doing up?" I demanded.

"I was waiting for you to come into my room and turn me into a rabbit," she replied. "Or pretend to, anyway."

"I'm not going to do that tonight," I said. "Go back to bed."

"What are *you* doing up? Where are you going?"

I sat on the front steps and pulled on my trainers. "Out to the garage," I lied. "To practise a new trick."

"You are not. I know where you're going. To Midnight Mansion!"

I grabbed her by the shoulders. "Okay. You're

161

right. I'm going to Midnight Mansion. Don't tell Mum and Dad—promise?"

"I want to go!" she insisted. "Let me go with you."

"No. Go back to bed—and don't tell. Or you'll be sorry."

"You *have* to take me!" she declared. "If you don't, I'll run upstairs and tell Mum and Dad right now. Then you'll never get to see Amaz-O."

"You wouldn't."

"I would."

I knew she would.

"All right," I agreed. "You can come. But you have to be good and do everything I tell you to do."

"Maybe I will—and maybe I won't."

I sighed. I had to take her, no matter how bratty she was. If I did, she'd never tell—because then she'd be in as much trouble as me.

"Let's go," I whispered.

We sneaked into the garage and got our bikes. Then we pedalled off into the night.

It felt strange riding down Bank Street late at night. The shops were all closed and dark. Hardly any traffic on the street.

Oh, no. A police car up ahead—driving towards us down Bank Street. If he spotted us, he'd stop us for sure. And then he'd take us home. And then we'd *really* be in trouble.

I searched desperately for a place to hide. The

police couldn't miss us—Bank Street was lined with streetlights.

"Ginny!" I called. "Quick—out of the light!" I swerved into the dark doorway of a dress shop. Ginny followed. We leaped off our bikes and pressed ourselves into the shadows.

The police car glided past. I held my breath as the headlights brushed across us. The car stopped.

"He saw us!" Ginny whispered. "Run!"

I grabbed her arm to stop her. "Wait." I peeked out into the street.

The police car was idling, but the driver stayed inside.

"It's a red light," I told Ginny. A few seconds later the light turned green, and the police car rolled away.

"We're safe now," I said. We hopped back on to our bikes and rode off.

Midnight Mansion loomed huge and dark at the edge of town. People said that a crazy old woman had lived alone in the mansion for forty years. She was rich, but so stingy she wore ragged old clothes and ate nothing but peanut butter, right out of the jar.

When people tried to visit her, she screamed, "Go away!" and threw rocks at them. She had about fifty cats. When she died, a businessman bought the mansion and turned it into a nightclub.

I braked in front of the old house and stared at it. Midnight Mansion.

It looked like a spooky old castle made of sooty black stone. Three storeys tall, with two towers shooting up into the night sky. Vines crept across the roof. A floodlight threw creepy shadows over the house.

I'd seen the mansion a million times before. But late at night it looked bigger and darker than usual. I thought I saw bats fluttering around the two towers.

"No wonder the old lady went crazy," Ginny whispered. "Living in a spooky place like that."

"Do you think she kept prisoners in those towers?" I wondered.

"I think she had a torture chamber in the basement," Ginny said.

We walked our bikes up to the entrance. People hurried inside to see Amaz-O's magic show. Three men in long black capes breezed past us. A woman with long black hair, black lipstick and pointy black fingernails smiled at me.

"Where did all these weird people come from?" Ginny asked.

I shrugged. "Let's go in. The show is about to start."

We locked our bikes and ran up the long stone steps. We entered a big hall lit by a crystal chandelier. We crossed the hall to a doorway covered by a heavy red curtain.

A tall, thin man in a black dinner-jacket guarded the curtain. He reached out a long, bony finger to stop us.

He had no hair, a pencil neck and dark, hollow eye sockets. "He looks like a skeleton," Ginny whispered to me.

I pulled the two tickets out of my back pocket and handed them to him.

"Very good," he croaked in a low voice. "But where are your parents? I can't seat children without their parents."

My parents? Think fast, Swanz-O, I told myself. "Um—my parents. Yes. Well, my parents, you see . . ." I had a feeling he didn't want to hear that my parents were at home sleeping.

"They're outside, parking the car," I lied. "They'll be here in a minute. They told us to come in and get a table."

The man's hollow black eyes seemed to burn a hole in my brain. Would he buy it?

"I don't like it. But all right." He led us through the red curtain. The houselights went down just as we walked in. He showed us to a table right next to the stage.

"Excellent!" I said to Ginny as we sat down. "The best seats in the whole place!"

"This is so exciting!" she exclaimed. "I can't believe we're in a real, grown-up nightclub. By ourselves!"

The eerie-looking host stood by the red curtain, watching us. "We may not be here long," I warned her. "That skeleton guy's got his eye on us. When he realizes we're not here with our parents—"

"Shh! The show's starting."

A voice came over a loudspeaker. "Ladies and gentlemen! Midnight Mansion is proud to present the most famous magician in America. The fabulous, the incredible, the mind-boggling Amaz-O!"

A drum roll, and then horns bleating. "Ta da!" The audience clapped and cheered. The curtain rose.

I gasped when I saw the stage. It was filled with wonderful equipment—a tall, shiny black box with a door in the front, a platform suspended from the ceiling, a glittering box with holes in it for a head, arms and legs to stick out of. And a big white rabbit sitting beside a vase of blue flowers on a table covered with a red scarf.

The rabbit wasn't tied up or caged or anything. "I wonder how he keeps that rabbit from running away," Ginny whispered. "That's a trick *you* need to learn."

"You're so funny, Ginny," I said, rolling my eyes. "My sides are splitting with laughter."

"You have no sense of humour," Ginny jeered. "That's your problem."

166

"No. *You're* my problem," I snapped.

Amaz-O strode on stage. He was tall and slim, and his top hat made him seem even taller. He had long black hair and wore a black cape lined with red satin over a black dinner-jacket.

He tossed the cape over his shoulders and bowed.

I can't believe I'm seeing Amaz-O in person! I thought, my heart pounding with excitement. And so close—I could almost touch him!

Maybe I'll even see how some of his tricks are done, I thought. Maybe, sitting so close, I'll catch some of his secrets!

Without saying a word, Amaz-O scanned the audience. He trained his eyes on me.

My whole body shook. He's staring right at me! I gasped.

Amaz-O took a step forward and leaned towards me.

What's he doing? I thought. Is he going to talk to me?

Amaz-O leaned closer. His face was right next to mine! I cowered in my seat.

He scowled and whispered in a deep, menacing voice, "Disappear! Disappear!"

I shrank back.

"Disappear!" he growled again.

"Excuse me?" I gasped. I stared up at him. On TV he seemed friendly. But in person he was definitely frightening.

"Disappear!" he whispered. "I'm going to make you disappear at the end of the show. I will ask for volunteers—and I will choose you."

He didn't want me to disappear for real. He wanted me to be part of his act! I couldn't believe it!

I'll find out how he does his famous disappearing trick! I thought. Maybe I'll get to meet him after the show. Maybe he'll even tell me some of his secrets!

Ginny leaned across the table. "He's going to make you disappear for ever!" she teased. "What will I tell Mum and Dad?"

I paid no attention to her. Nothing Ginny did or said could bother me now.

This was too cool! Just seeing Amaz-O was exciting enough. But he chose *me* to be in his show!

Maybe he could tell that I'm a magician, too, I thought.

Amaz-O began his act. "Good evening, ladies and gentlemen," he crooned. "Tonight you will see some amazing feats. You will see me do things you always thought were impossible. Are these feats real—or are they illusions? It's up to you to decide."

He waved his hands, and a wand appeared out of thin air. The audience clapped.

Then Amaz-O began to fidget with his hat, as if it felt uncomfortable on his head. "Something is wrong with my hat," he said. "It feels strange—almost as if. . ."

He lifted the hat off his head and peered into it. He showed us the inside of it. It looked perfectly normal. There was nothing inside it.

He placed it back on his head. "It's funny," he chuckled. "I thought for a minute there might be something inside my hat. I thought I felt— oh, I don't know—a flock of birds fluttering around in there."

The hat jiggled. Amaz-O appeared annoyed. "There it goes again!"

He whipped the hat off his head and stared into it. On top of his head sat a large white feather. People in the audience giggled.

"What's so funny?" Amaz-O asked. He felt the top of his head and found the feather. "Where did that come from?" he gasped, acting amazed. Everyone laughed.

"Well, I'll try not to let this bother me," he went on, replacing his hat. "Back to the show. For my first trick—"

The hat began to shake again—slightly at first, then harder. It practically jumped off his head. The audience cracked up. Amaz-O pretended to be horrified.

He yanked the hat off his head—and out flew a whole flock of doves! They swooped over the audience and flew up to the rafters.

"I *knew* something was going on in there!" Amaz-O joked. Loud laughter and clapping.

He's the greatest, I thought, clapping along. How did he get all those birds inside his hat?

I glanced at the rabbit on stage. It sat calmly on the table, staring at Amaz-O. It almost seemed to be watching the act.

I can't wait to see his rabbit trick, I thought. Will he make the rabbit disappear? Or pull off some kind of twist?

"For my next trick I need a needle and thread," Amaz-O announced. He produced a packet of needles and a long, thick thread from one of his pockets. He picked out a needle and squinted, trying to push the thread through the eye.

"I always have trouble threading a needle," he said. He licked the end of the thread and tried again. He couldn't get the thread to go through.

He threw up his hands in frustration. "It's impossible!" he cried. "How do tailors do it?"

The audience chuckled. I waited to see what would come next. I knew all this needle-and-thread business was a build-up to something incredible.

"So much for the *hard* way to thread a needle," Amaz-O said. "I'll show you a better way."

He snatched up the packet of needles. There must have been at least twenty needles stuck into a piece of cardboard. He popped the whole thing into his mouth. Then he dangled the long string over his mouth like a piece of spaghetti.

He slowly drew the string into his mouth, chewing. It looked as if he were eating a piece of spaghetti—with a packet of needles in his mouth, too.

"Don't you think that hurts?" Ginny whispered. "Chewing up all those needles?"

I barely nodded. I watched Amaz-O, spellbound.

Amaz-O nearly swallowed the whole string. A few centimetres of string stuck out between his lips. The audience waited, hushed.

He paused. Then he opened his mouth and tugged at the string. Slowly, slowly, he pulled it out of his mouth.

171

One by one the needles appeared—dangling from the string! Somehow he had threaded twenty needles with his tongue!

The audience gasped, then applauded. The needles flashed as Amaz-O held up the string.

"Threading needles the easy way!" he cried as he took another bow.

I've got to find out how he did that, I thought. Maybe I'll ask him after the show.

"How's the show going?" Amaz-O asked the audience. We all cheered. "I wonder how much time we have left?" He strode across the stage to the table where the rabbit and the blue flowers sat on top of the red scarf.

With a flick of his wrist, he yanked his scarf out from under the rabbit.

The rabbit didn't move. Neither did the vase of flowers. The table was now bare.

The rabbit blinked calmly. Amaz-O waved the scarf over his left hand. He let it drop—and a big red alarm clock appeared in his hand!

He glanced at the clock. "I suppose we have time for a few more tricks." He covered the clock with the scarf—and the clock disappeared.

A loud ringing suddenly erupted from the other side of the stage. I turned towards it.

The red alarm clock—floating in mid-air! It seemed to have flown across the stage by itself.

Amaz-O crossed the stage, grabbed the clock, and shut off the alarm.

"My clock is a little fast," he joked. "It's not time for the show to end. Not yet."

I hope not, I thought. This is the greatest magic act I've ever seen in my life!

The rest of the show was fantastic, too. Amaz-O escaped from a locked safe. He walked through a brick wall. He tapped his hat with his magic wand—and in a puff of smoke his dinner-jacket changed from black to yellow!

"And now for my big finale," Amaz-O announced. "I am going to make a member of the audience disappear. Are there any volunteers?"

He gazed out over the audience. No one said a word. Ginny kicked me under the table.

"Ow!" I whispered, rubbing my skin. "What did you do that for?"

"He asked for *volunteers*, you moron," she said. "That means you."

I'd been so caught up in the show, I almost forgot. I stood up. "I'd like to volunteer."

Amaz-O smiled. "Excellent, young man. Please step up on stage."

My stomach suddenly jolted with terror. I stumbled up to the stage.

Here I go, I thought nervously. Amaz-O is going to make me disappear.

I hope nothing goes wrong.

Amaz-O towered over me on stage. This is unbelievable, I thought. I'm on stage with the great
Amaz-O. I'm about to be part of one of his
famous tricks.

He's going to make me disappear!

I clutched my stomach, wondering, why do I
feel so scared?

"Thanks for volunteering, young man,"
Amaz-O said to me. "You must be very brave.
Are your parents here tonight?"

My parents? Uh-oh. "Um—they're here. Sure
they're here," I stammered. "But—uh—they
had to make a phone call."

Amaz-O frowned. "A phone call? In the middle
of my show?"

"Well—it was an emergency," I explained.

"Never mind. I'm glad they've stepped away.
If they knew what was about to happen to you,
they might try to stop me."

174

"Stop you?" My heart skittered nervously. But I heard the audience laughing.

Don't let him scare you, I told myself. This is just part of the act. He's joking.

I faked a laugh. "What—um—exactly—is about to happen to me?"

"I'm going to make you disappear," Amaz-O replied. "You will be transported into another dimension. I will try my best to bring you back, of course—but it doesn't *always* work."

"It doesn't?" I gulped.

He patted me on the back. "Don't worry. I've done this hundreds of times. I've only missed once or twice."

The audience chuckled. They figured he was kidding. I hoped they were right.

"Is that your sister sitting at the front table?" Amaz-O asked.

I nodded.

"Better wave goodbye to her, just in case," he warned me.

Ginny smiled and waved at me.

She can't *wait* for me to disappear! I thought bitterly. She hopes I'll never come back.

"Go on," Amaz-O urged. "Wave to her."

I smiled weakly and waved at Ginny. The audience laughed. Then Amaz-O led me to a tall black box in the centre of the stage. He threw open the door. It looked like a cupboard inside.

175

"Step inside here if you would, please," he said.

I stepped inside the box. Amaz-O shut the door firmly.

It was pitch-black inside that box. I stood still, waiting for something to happen. I could hear Amaz-O talking to the audience.

"Ladies and gentlemen, this box is my own invention—the Fifth Dimension Spin-o-Rama." I heard him slap his hand against the side of the box.

"Here's how it works: my brave volunteer steps inside the box. I lock him in. I spin the box ten times—*very* fast.

"A magical force inside the box will send the boy into another dimension. He will disappear!

"I must ask for absolute silence while I do this trick. I need complete concentration."

For several seconds I heard nothing.

Then the box began to spin. "Whoa!" I cried. My body slammed against the back of the box.

It whirled around faster than any ride in an amusement park. I shut my eyes. I felt so dizzy.

I hope I don't puke, I thought. That would spoil everything.

The box kept spinning, spinning. How will the trick work? I wondered. How will I disappear?

What if he really sends me into another dimension?

But that's just talk, I told myself. Magician talk—to entertain the audience.

Isn't it?

The box spun faster and faster. I clutched my stomach. I saw stars dancing before my eyes.

When is it going to stop? I thought. I'm really going to be sick.

Then, suddenly, the bottom of the box dropped out from under me.

"Help!" I cried as I fell down, down, down.

"Whoa!"

I slid down a long wooden chute and landed—*thunk!*—on some kind of mattress.

I lay on my back in a daze. I heard water dripping somewhere. A dim yellow light flickered from a bare bulb on the ceiling.

I sat up, gazing around me. The room was nearly empty, dark and damp, with a cement floor. I spotted a furnace in the corner.

I'm in the basement of Midnight Mansion, I realized.

I stood up and examined the chute. So that's how the trick works, I thought. Amaz-O sets up his spinning box over a trapdoor in the floor of the stage. The bottom of the box drops out, and the volunteer slides down the chute and out of sight. When Amaz-O opens the door of the box—*presto!*—the volunteer has disappeared. It's so simple.

But how do I get back upstairs? I wondered. How will Amaz-O make me reappear?

Muffled applause drifted down from overhead. I could hear Amaz-O's voice, faintly. "Thank you very much, ladies and gentlemen. I must be going now. I've got to disappear into the fifth dimension and find that boy! Good night!"

The audience laughed. Then I heard music, an explosion, and loud clapping.

Amaz-O must have made himself disappear, I thought. He'll probably come sliding down this chute any minute.

I waited.

No one came sliding down the chute.

I waited a few more minutes.

Nothing.

He must have disappeared some other way, I figured.

He'll show up soon, I thought. He'll come and let me out of here. And then I'll ask him how he does that trick with the alarm clock. Maybe he'll even give me his autograph!

A few minutes later I heard chairs scraping across the floor upstairs and a stampede of footsteps. The show was over. The audience was leaving.

Is somebody going to let me out of here? I wondered. I was getting a little nervous. I sat down on the mattress to wait.

What's taking Amaz-O so long?

Maybe he wants to wait until everyone is gone, so no one will figure out how he did the trick. That must be it.

I waited a little longer. I heard a rustling, scuttling noise. A rat! I thought, jumping up off the mattress. I stared at the floor, watching for the rat.

The noise stopped.

Maybe it wasn't a rat, I thought, trying to calm myself. My muscles were all tense. Maybe it was only a mouse. Or a cockroach. Or my imagination.

The *drip, drip, drip* of the water somewhere in the basement was starting to drive me crazy. *Drip, drip, drip*. Like some kind of water torture.

Where is Amaz-O? When is he going to let me out of here?

I listened for signs of life upstairs. Nothing. Everything was silent up there now.

Okay, I said to myself. Everyone is gone. You can let me out now, Amaz-O.

I listened hard. I didn't hear anyone in the building.

What if Amaz-O is gone, too? I thought, panicking. What if he's forgotten about me and left me here?

I've got to find a way out myself, I decided.

I crept across the cement floor, keeping an eye out for rats.

It sure is dark down here, I thought.

I drifted towards the dripping sound and found myself in a room with a big laundry sink. I crossed the laundry room. On the other side I found a steep flight of steps leading to a door at the top.

Aha, I thought, feeling better now. A way out.

I climbed the rickety stairs. I reached for the doorknob and pushed.

The door didn't open. I turned the knob again and pulled.

Nothing.

The door was locked!

I rattled the door as hard as I could. I pounded on it with my fists.

"Let me out of here!" I cried. "Can anyone hear me?

"Let me out of here!"

"Hey!" I shouted. I rattled the door. "Somebody! Get me out of here!"

How could Amaz-O do this? I thought angrily. How could he forget all about me like this?

He wouldn't lock me in the basement on purpose—would he?

No, I told myself. Why would he want to do that?

It's all just a big mistake.

I shook the door again. It loosened a little. I pushed on it, and it opened a crack.

The door was bolted from the outside with a metal hook. But the hook wasn't secure.

I'll bet I can break the door open, I realized.

I backed part of the way down the stairs. Then I ran to the top and threw myself against the door.

"Ow!" I grunted. The door loosened a little more. But it didn't open. And now my shoulder ached.

Then I thought the unthinkable. I couldn't believe I was thinking this—but I sure wished Ginny were with me.

She could've karate-kicked through that door in about five seconds. I know, because she's kicked her way into my bedroom lots of times.

Where is Ginny, anyway? I thought. She must be outside in the car park, waiting for me.

I had to try again. I rammed my shoulder against the door as hard as I could.

Bang! The hook broke, and the door flew open.

Excellent, I thought, rubbing my shoulder. I'm out of that horrible basement at last.

But where am I now?

A long, dark corridor.

"Hello?" I called. No answer. "Hello?"

Where is everybody? I wondered. Shouldn't there be stage-hands bustling around or something?

I tiptoed down the hall. The place appeared deserted.

How could they have left me down in the basement like that? I thought angrily. How could they leave me here alone—and just go home?

At the end of the hall I saw a sliver of light. It came from under a door.

Someone's still here, I realized. Maybe it's Amaz-O!

I crept down the hall. The door had a star on it. It must be Amaz-O's dressing room! I thought. This is fantastic! I'm alone in Midnight Mansion with the great Amaz-O! We'll probably stay up all night talking about magic. If I could get him to show me a few of his secrets. . .

I felt so excited and nervous my hands shook. I almost forgot about being left in the basement.

That was just a mistake, I thought. A stagehand forgot to come and get me. Amaz-O must have thought I was all right. He'll probably be really glad to see me.

I stared at the star on the door. What should I do? I wondered. Should I knock? Should I call out his name?

I'll knock, I decided. I stepped to the door. *Thunk!* I tripped over something propped against the wall. A large black case with PROPERTY OF AMAZ-O written on the side.

Wow, I thought, running my fingers along the gold letters. This must be Amaz-O's magic kit! I'm touching it with my own hands!

I turned back to the door. I was about to meet my idol, my all-time hero. It was the biggest moment of my life.

I reached for the door. My hand trembled. I knocked lightly.

I waited.

Maybe he didn't hear me, I thought. I knocked again, harder this time.

Nothing.

"Hello?" I called softly, peeking into the room.

Amaz-O's big white rabbit perched on the couch. Amaz-O sat on a chair across from the rabbit. I could see his legs.

"Hello?" I called again. "It's me. From the disappearing act. Can I come in?"

I paused at the door. Amaz-O didn't answer me. Suddenly the door slammed shut in my face!

"Hey!" I cried in surprise.

A voice growled at me from the other side. "Beat it!"

"But—I'm your biggest fan! I'd just like to shake hands—"

"Beat it!" the voice snarled again. "Beat it, punk!"

Punk? *Punk?*

Did the great Amaz-O call me a punk?

I couldn't believe it. I stood staring at the star on the door in shock.

How could Amaz-O talk to me this way? After I volunteered for his disappearing trick—and he left me locked in the basement!

What's his *problem*, anyway?

For a few seconds I couldn't move. I couldn't think. My hero had called me a punk. The greatest magician in the world—and he turned out to be a big fat jerk!

Okay, so he wasn't fat. But he was the biggest jerk I'd ever met in my whole life.

I hung my head and turned away from the door to leave. Then I saw it again—the big black case.

Amaz-O's magic kit.

Without thinking, I grabbed the case and ran. It was heavy and awkward, but I lugged it down the hall as quickly and quietly as I could.

Why am I doing this? I wondered as I burst into the stage area.

I'm still not sure why I did it. I'd gone through so much trouble to get to the show—sneaking out of the house to meet Amaz-O. And then he was so mean to me. Maybe I wanted to get back at him.

It doesn't matter why I did it. I did it. I stole Amaz-O's magic tricks.

In the back of my mind, I knew I was heading for trouble.

I paused near the stage. Was Amaz-O following me? I listened.

Not a sound. No one coming. I swallowed hard and started running again.

I passed under the chandelier in the lobby and burst through the front door. I hope Amaz-O was the last person in the club, I thought. I hope there aren't any guards lurking around.

I didn't have time to check. I dragged the case across the gravel car park towards my bike.

Almost there, I told myself, panting. The car park was empty now. The floodlights that lit up the mansion were off. The old house lay hidden in darkness.

It must be really late, I thought. I'd better hurry home.

My bike stood where I'd left it, leaning against a rail.

I was reaching for the handlebars when a voice called, "Stop!"

I froze.

I knew I was caught.

I heard heavy footsteps crunch towards me across the gravel car park.

Here they come, I thought. They've caught me red-handed with Amaz-O's bag. They'll probably arrest me.

"Where were you?" the voice called.

Ginny! I'd completely forgotten about her. Oops.

"Why are you leaving without me?" she demanded.

"Wh-why?" I stammered. What could I say? I didn't want to admit I'd forgotten all about her. "I-I wasn't leaving without you. I was looking for you. Where have *you* been?"

"Looking for *you*, Tim," she snapped. "What happened to you? You disappeared—and you never came back!"

"It's a long story," I said.

She leaned forward to read the lettering on

Amaz-O's black case. "'Property of Amaz-O.' Where did you get that?"

"He gave it to me," I lied. "Wasn't that nice of him?"

She reached out to open the clasp that held the case shut. "Cool. What's inside?"

I stopped her hand. "I'll show it to you when we get home. It's filled with tricks. Amaz-O said I could keep it. He was grateful to me for being such a good sport in the disappearing act."

Ginny looked puzzled. "If Amaz-O gave you that case," she began, "why are those guards running this way?"

I glanced towards the mansion. Two guards charged across the car park, waving torches. Uh-oh.

I grabbed the case. "Let's get out of here!" I cried. "Quick—get on your bike. Let's ride!"

"I can't!" Ginny cried.

"Huh? Why not?"

"My bike's gone!"

I jumped on my bike. "Too bad!" I cried. "See you at home!"

"Tim!" Ginny wailed. "You can't leave me here!"

I would have left her there if I could. She can take care of herself. But I knew Mum and Dad would kill me.

Besides, when the guards caught her, she'd tell on me. I'd still get in trouble.

I sat on my bike, watching the guards run right for us. Then I spotted her bike on the edge of the car park. "It's over there!" I told her. "Hurry!"

She raced to her bike. I balanced the case on top of my handlebars. It wasn't easy.

"Stop!" a guard yelled. Ginny and I sped out of the car park and down the dark street.

"Hey—stop!" the guards shouted. The beams of their torches blinded me for a second. I pedalled as hard as I could. Ginny darted ahead of me.

I clutched the black case with one hand and steered with the other. The case slowed me down. The guards were gaining on us. At the first corner I zoomed left. Ginny followed.

I glanced back. The guards had stopped running. One of them bent over, panting.

"They'll never catch us now!" Ginny shouted. We biked home as fast as we could. The streets were empty and really dark. The lights were out in most of the houses.

It's after midnight, I realized. Please let Mum and Dad be asleep. If they catch us, they'll ground us till we're thirty-five! I'd almost rather be arrested.

But then, if I got arrested, Mum and Dad would *still* ground me.

We braked at our street and walked our bikes into the driveway.

"Sshhh," Ginny whispered.

"Sshhh yourself," I whispered back.

We parked the bikes in the garage. It was hard to see without the lights on. On the way into the house, Ginny tripped over the lawn mower.

"Ow!" she yelped.

"Quiet!" I snapped.

We both froze. Did Mum and Dad hear us? Silence. "I think it's okay," I whispered.

"That hurt," Ginny whined.

"Ssshhhh!"

We sneaked into the house. "I'll hide the case in my room," I whispered.

"I want to look at it now," Ginny protested.

I shook my head. "It's mine."

"No, it's not. You have to share it with me."

"Amaz-O gave it to *me*," I insisted, even though it wasn't exactly true.

"I'm going to tell Mum and Dad," Ginny threatened. "I'll tell them you woke me up and forced me to go with you to Midnight Mansion."

"You little brat!" I cried angrily. Stupid Ginny. "Okay, I'll share it with you."

"Promise?"

"If you promise not to tell Mum and Dad."

"I promise. But you can't keep the case in your room. It's both of ours now."

I sighed. "All right. I'll hide it in the attic. Okay?"

She nodded.

"But we won't touch it until Saturday," I said. "On Saturday, we'll have plenty of time to try everything out and do it right. Deal?"

"Deal. On Saturday we'll *both* open the case, at the same time, *together*."

"Right. Now go to bed. I'll sneak it up to the attic."

We tried to be careful going up the creaky stairs. It took us about ten minutes. At the top

I paused to listen for sounds from Mum and Dad's room.

"Everything is okay," Ginny whispered. "Dad is snoring."

She crept into her room and shut the door. I tiptoed up to the attic, lugging the black case.

I shut the attic door and switched on the light. Where can I hide this? I wondered, gazing around at all the junk. I stepped over piles of old magazines. In one corner sat my old toy chest.

Perfect, I thought, opening the chest. I pulled out a toy school bus and a couple of trucks to make room for the case.

What's in here, anyway? I wondered as I hefted Amaz-O's case. I held Amaz-O's magic kit in my hands. How could I go to sleep without seeing what's in it? How could I wait two whole days until Saturday?

Maybe I'll take a little peek inside, I thought. Just a quick one. Then I'll go to bed.

I set the case on the floor. My hands trembled as I fumbled with the clasp.

Here goes, I thought, tugging open the clasp. I pulled the case open—

And it blew up in my face!

I fell over backwards. I lay sprawled on the floor, covering my eyes.

What happened?

Am I dead?

I opened my eyes. I squeezed my arms. I grabbed my chest.

I'm okay, I realized.

I sat up. The case sat on the floor. No signs of an explosion.

Carefully I crawled over to the case. I could have sworn it had blown up. But I didn't see anything that would blow up.

Then, taped to the inside of the top flap, I saw a little metal disk. I tapped it. It made a muffled roar.

I examined the metal disk. It was an electronic chip. It made an explosion sound effect when I shook it or tapped it.

Just one of Amaz-O's tricks.

What else is in here? I wondered.

I pulled out all kinds of cool stuff. A pair of trick handcuffs. A pocket watch for hypnotizing people. Three different packs of trick cards. A rope. And a long chain of silk scarves tied together.

I wonder how all this stuff works, I thought. I'll have to fool around with it on Saturday and figure it out.

I found a small black sack that held three oval shells and a little red ball. The shell game, I realized. One of my favourite tricks. You hide the ball under one of the shells and shift them around. The audience has to guess which shell the ball is under.

They always guess wrong, because the ball isn't under *any* of the shells. The magician secretly palms the ball while he's shifting the shells around.

Gets 'em every time.

I reached into the case again. My hand brushed against something silky. I pulled it out. It was a black dinner-jacket.

"Wow!" I gasped. "Amaz-O's own jacket!"

I had to try it on. I pulled it over my shoulders. It was too big. The shoulders drooped halfway down my arms, and the sleeves covered my hands.

But it felt great. I ran my hands over the satin lapels.

I stood up and walked around in it. A real

magician's jacket. I wonder what he's got in the pockets?

I stuck my hands in the pockets. But suddenly I felt something wiggle. Along the back of the jacket, near the neck.

I shook my shoulders. The wiggling stopped.

But then I felt it again. Something came sliding down the sleeve!

I shook my arm. What is it? I thought. Is it alive?

The thing crawled along my arm. "Yuck!" I sputtered. "Get off me!" I squirmed inside the coat, trying to shake the thing off.

I had to get the jacket off—straight away! I struggled to get my arms out of the sleeves.

Then something poked its head out. Out of the sleeve, near my hand.

A snake.

A live snake.

I clamped my mouth shut to keep from screaming. The snake felt warm and creepy against my
arm. I shook my arm hard. The snake clung to
me!

I gritted my teeth and shook my arm again.
And again. I brushed at my sleeve with my free
hand.

It wasn't working!

I shook my arm once more, as hard as I could.
The snake uncoiled and slithered out of the
sleeve. It dropped to the floor.

It hissed and curved around the toy chest. I
watched it with a shiver.

Then I felt it again—that slippery, wriggling
feeling. Something hissed near my ear and
squirmed across my shoulder.

"Ohhh!" I moaned. Another snake! I slapped
at it. "Get off me!"

As I tried to brush the snake away, another
one slithered down my sleeve. Something slimy

wriggled across my stomach and down my back. A snake popped out of an inner pocket and plopped to the floor. It started to coil around my leg.

The jacket is crammed with snakes! I realized with horror.

I thrashed my arms, frantically trying to tear off the jacket. A snake slid down the front of my shirt.

I thrashed harder, shaking my arms and legs. Now I was covered with snakes! My whole body!

I wanted to scream—but I couldn't wake Mum and Dad. A snake curled up my neck and around my head. I squirmed, desperately trying to get out of the jacket.

"Help!" I moaned. "Ohhhh—help!"

Snakes everywhere!

One slithered over my head. With a trembling hand, I grabbed at it and heaved it away.

Gasping in terror, I struggled out of the jacket. I tossed it on the floor. Snakes wriggled over it. Snakes wriggled over my feet. I hopped up and down. Then I hopped on to a chair. A snake coiled up the leg of the chair. It crept closer. "Go away!" I whispered. "Leave me alone!"

The snake hissed. I jumped off the chair.

Squish! My stomach turned. Did I step on a snake? I was afraid to look.

I lifted my foot and glanced down. I hadn't stepped on a snake. It was one of Ginny's old dolls.

A snake slid over the doll's face and around its neck. Another snake slithered over my shoe.

There's no escape! I realized. I've got no

choice—I have to wake up Mum and Dad. What else can I do?

I hopped around the squirming, hissing snakes. I'll get into trouble, I thought. But at least I'll be out of this snake pit!

A snake darted towards me—then suddenly froze. The room fell silent. No more hissing.

All around me the snakes stopped moving. They lay stiff on the floor. Their cold eyes stared.

What happened? Were they dead?

I glanced around, afraid to move. The floor was littered with dead snakes.

How could they all die at once? I wondered. It's so weird!

I stood there, not moving a muscle. My eyes darted around the room.

I slowly reached out my leg and tapped one of the snakes with my foot. It jiggled a little.

I took a deep breath. Should I touch it?

I got up the courage to bend close to the snake. I stuck out a finger and poked at it. Nothing happened. My heart pounded. I picked up the snake.

It lay limp in my hand. It didn't seem real.

I twisted the body. It was rubber! I examined the eyes. They were made of glass.

They're mechanical snakes, I realized.

I turned the snake over. I found a tiny wind-up key hidden under a rubber flap.

Amaz-O's jacket was rigged with wind-up snakes.

I began to breathe again. Everything is okay, I told myself. I don't have to wake up Mum and Dad. I'm not going to get into trouble. I'm not going to be eaten alive by snakes.

When will I learn? I scolded myself. *All* of these things are just tricks. None of them is real. Amaz-O is a magician.

I gathered up the snakes and stuffed them back inside the jacket. Then I jammed the jacket into Amaz-O's magic kit. I took one last look inside the bag.

This is amazing, I thought. I've got some of Amaz-O's best tricks—right here in my own house!

I forced myself to close the kit. I'd better stop fooling around with this stuff, I thought—before anything else happens!

I'll check it all out on Saturday. In daylight, when I have plenty of time to see how it all works.

Then I'll give the kit back to Amaz-O. On Monday.

I knew I had to return the kit. It had been wrong to take it. And crazy.

If only Amaz-O hadn't been so mean to me! He used me in his act—and then he locked me in the basement! He told me to get lost. He called me a punk!

I started to get angry all over again. Amaz-O doesn't deserve to get his magic kit back, I thought.

But deep down I knew I had to return it. I wanted to do the right thing. I'd check out the tricks, then give them back.

Of course, I didn't know then how dangerous the kit was. I didn't know the trouble it would cause.

If I had known, I would have returned the case *that night*!

"Another day of work," Mum sighed at the breakfast table the next morning. "I'm absolutely dreading it. Those students just drive me crazy."

Dad grabbed a doughnut and gazed out the window. "It's raining," he said unhappily. "I probably won't sell a single car today."

Ginny and I exchanged glances. Mum and Dad had no idea we had sneaked out the night before.

I slumped into a chair and ate my cereal. I was sleepy. I'm not used to staying up so late.

"You look tired, Tim," Mum said, sitting across from me. She glanced at Ginny. "So do you, honey."

"Didn't you two get any sleep?" Dad asked.

"Sure we did," I replied.

Ginny grinned. "Not that much sleep. Tim and I have a secret!"

The little brat! I kicked her under the table.

"Ow!" she cried. "Tim kicked me!"

"Don't kick your sister," Dad scolded. "I have to leave." He picked up his briefcase and kissed Mum goodbye. "Off to another day of torture. See you tonight, kids."

Dad left. Mum started clearing away the breakfast dishes. "Did you say something about a secret?" she asked.

"No!" I insisted. "Ginny didn't say anything about a secret. She said, 'Tim and I want a wee pet.'"

Mum shot me a weird look. "A what? A wee pet?"

"Yeah," I said. "You know, a little pet. A nice little kitten or something. Ginny's learning about Scotland in school now. She's picked up some Scottish words, right, Ginny? She's been running around calling everything 'wee'."

"I have not," Ginny protested. "I've never called anything 'wee' in my life! And I'm not learning about Scotland in school!"

"Yes, you *are*," I insisted.

"What in the world are you two talking about?" Mum carried the pile of cereal bowls to the sink.

"We did a bad thing, Mum," Ginny blurted out. "Ow!" I kicked her again, but that didn't stop her.

"We sneaked out last night, Mum. We rode our bikes to Midnight Mansion to see the magic show. We didn't get back until after midnight. I'm sorry, Mum. Please don't get angry. Tim made me do it. I didn't want to."

I covered my face with my hands. Why does Ginny have to be such a big mouth?

I'm doomed, I thought. *Doomed!*

"What did you say, Ginny?" Mum asked, wiping her hands on a towel. "I was running water in the sink, and I couldn't hear you."

I let out a long breath. I couldn't believe my luck. I glared at Ginny and kicked her again—really hard this time.

"Nothing, Mum," Ginny murmured. "I didn't say anything."

"You two better get ready for school," Mum said.

I pushed my chair away from the table and dragged Ginny out of hers. "We'll be ready in a minute, Mum," I said.

"What is your problem?" I whispered to Ginny in the hall. "You could've got us in big trouble!"

"*You* would get in trouble. Not me," Ginny replied. "You're the big brother. You *made* me go."

"I didn't make you do anything. And anyway, you promised not to tell!"

"You promised not to peek into Amaz-O's kit until Saturday," Ginny reminded me. "But I sneaked up to the attic this morning—and I know you looked! You opened that bag! You even played with some of the stuff!"

"Me? I did not!" I lied.

"Yes, you did. One of the sleeves of a jacket was sticking out of the kit. And I found a scarf on the floor. You big fat liar!"

"So what? You'll still get to see the stuff on Saturday."

"You promised," Ginny repeated. She flicked my nose. "Boi-oi-oing."

I stormed into my room. There's no arguing with Ginny. She does whatever she wants—promise or no promise.

She's always getting me into trouble, I thought angrily. She drives me crazy! I wish there were some way I could pay her back. Some way to pay her back for everything.

Little did I realize I would soon find it.

"Are you sure you kids don't want to go to the antiques show with us?" Dad asked. "You might see some neat old junk there."

"We're sure," I insisted. Saturday morning had arrived, and all I could think about was Amaz-O's magic kit. I couldn't wait to get my hands on it.

I wished my parents would hurry up and leave.

"All right," Mum said, kissing Ginny and then me. "There's tuna salad in the fridge for lunch. We won't be back until dinnertime."

"Be good," Dad added.

"*I'll* be good," Ginny declared. "I don't know about *Tim*."

I tried to shove her, but she dodged me. "I'll be good," I promised. "I'm always good."

Mum rolled her eyes. "Just don't fight too much," she said. "'Bye."

Ah. At last. As soon as they were gone, I raced to the phone and rang Foz's number.

"The coast is clear," I told him. "Come on over."

I'd told Foz all about the show at Midnight Mansion and Amaz-O's magic kit. He begged me to let him see the cool tricks in Amaz-O's bag.

As soon as Foz arrived, we all trooped up to the attic. Ginny made a beeline for the magic kit. I blocked her.

"Heeee-ya!" She leaped into a pre-karate chop stance. "Out of my way!"

"Ginny—wait!" I pleaded. "There's a lot of weird stuff in that bag. Let me show it to you my way."

"Okay." She relaxed. "But don't forget you're supposed to share it with me."

I pulled up two chairs. "You guys sit here," I said to Ginny and Foz. "And get ready for the greatest magic show in the history of the world!"

I reached into the toy chest and pulled out Amaz-O's magic kit. I held it up in front of Foz and Ginny. "First," I began in my magician voice, "gaze deeply into the magic trove."

I held the bag near their faces. They stared at it. I yanked it open.

Kaboom! It made the exploding sound, just as it did the first time I opened it.

Ginny and Foz fell off their chairs!

"What happened?" Foz moaned, clutching his head. "That thing blew up in my face!"

I cracked up. "It's only a sound effect," I explained.

"Not funny," Ginny complained.

"You should have seen your faces," I said gleefully. I reached into the black sack that held the three shells and the red ball. I set the shells in a row on a small table.

"Watch closely," I said. I held up the red ball. "See this ball? I'll place it under one of these shells." I pretended to tuck the ball under the middle shell. But secretly I palmed the ball and flicked it up my sleeve.

I began moving the shells over the table, shifting their places.

"Keep your eyes on the middle shell," I instructed. Then I stopped moving the shells.

"Which shell is the ball under?" I asked.

"That one," Ginny said, pointing to the shell on the right.

"Are you *sure*?" I prompted. "Foz, where do you think the ball is?"

"The same one as Ginny," he said. "I watched it the whole time."

"If you say so," I said. I was sure the ball wasn't under that shell—it wasn't under any of them. I felt the ball rubbing against my wrist.

I lifted the shell—and gasped. There *was* a ball under there. A red ball, just like the one I'd palmed.

211

"I was right!" Ginny crowed. "That's a stupid trick."

"But this is impossible!" I cried. I let the first ball fall out of my sleeve. I *had* palmed it.

"This is very strange," I muttered. "Let me try again."

I dropped the first ball on the floor. I picked up the second ball and pretended to slip it under a different shell. I palmed the ball and tucked it up my sleeve again.

"Here we go," I said, shifting the shells all over the table. I slid the shells around a little longer, then stopped.

"The ball is under the first shell," Foz said.

"Yes, the first shell," Ginny agreed.

"This time you're wrong!" I cried. I lifted the first shell. Another red ball!

Ginny sneered. "You're a real ace, Tim."

"Wait a second," I said. I lifted up the other two shells. All three of them had red balls under them!

"This isn't working at all," I grumbled. I set the shells down, then lifted them again. More balls! There were now three balls under each shell!

"This isn't the shell game I know." I was mystified. "This must be some other trick."

"It's way better than your dumb trick," Ginny said. "Those balls are coming out of nowhere!"

The shells began to dance as balls bubbled out

of them like popcorn. Ten balls. Twenty balls. Little red balls covered the table and bounced to the floor.

"They're still coming!" Foz cried in amazement. "We're going to be up to our necks in red balls!"

How do I stop this thing? I wondered.

Can I stop it?

21

I snatched up the shells and tossed them into their black sack. Then I grabbed all the red balls I could and stuffed them in, too.

"Help me, you guys!" I pleaded.

Ginny and Foz fell to their knees, gathering up red balls. We shoved them all into the sack. I pulled the string that closed it and dropped it into the magic kit.

The black sack kept bubbling. Red balls started bursting out of it.

"Stop that!" I yelled. I reached into the magic case and pulled out the first thing I touched. Then I snapped the case shut.

"I don't really get that trick," Ginny complained.

"Here's another trick," I said. "This one will be better." In my hand I held a flattened top hat. "Let's see what this does."

I punched the top hat open and placed it on my head.

"It's just a hat," Foz said, fidgeting. "It's kind of hot up here. Can we go down to the kitchen and get something to eat?"

"You guys don't get it," I said. "This is *Amaz-O*'s magic case! Okay, so I don't know how anything works yet. Once we figure it out, we could put on the best magic show ever! I could become a famous magician!"

"And I could be a famous magician's sister." Ginny yawned. "Big deal."

"That hat looks way cool on you," Foz said. "Now can we get something to eat?"

"I'm hungry, too," Ginny added.

"Wait!" I cried. I felt something move under the hat. I whipped it off.

"A white dove!" Foz cried.

"That's a good trick," Ginny admitted.

I shook the dove off my head. "How do you get it back in the hat?" I asked. Before I had a chance to try, another dove popped out of the hat.

I set the second dove on the floor. "There's another one!" Foz shouted.

A third dove flew out of the hat and settled on top of an old lamp. Out popped a fourth, and a fifth. . .

Foz started laughing. "These tricks are totally out of control!"

"This is no joke, Foz!" I snapped.

"We're going to be in major trouble," Ginny

warned. "We've got to find a way to get rid of these birds."

The attic was quickly filling up with flapping fluttering doves—and they kept coming. I knew we had to get rid of them—but how?

"Maybe there's something in here that will help." I ripped open the magic case. *Kaboom!* It made that stupid exploding sound again. Dozens of little red balls flew into my face.

"I'm really getting sick of this," I muttered.

I brushed away piles of balls. I pulled out a long black stick with a white tip. A magic wand!

"Maybe this will help!" I cried. I hoped it would. The attic was a total mess—white doves and red balls everywhere.

"This is the answer," I declared. "Amaz-O probably uses this wand to make the magic stop."

"I hope you're right," Ginny said. "If that doesn't work, you and I are going to have to run away from home."

"It'll work," I insisted. "It's got to."

I waved the wand in the air. "Stop!" I shouted. "Everything stop!"

Did it work?

No.

More doves flew out of the hat. More red balls bubbled out of the black sack.

"That magic wand is the only thing in there that *doesn't* work!" Foz joked.

"Be quiet!" I snapped. "I've got to think!"

"Yikes!" Ginny screamed. "A snake!"

She pointed at the magic case. A snake slithered out of it. Then a second, a third.

The mechanical snakes had come back to life!

Hissing snakes soon covered the floor, wriggling over the bouncing red balls. Dove feathers fell from the ceiling. The attic was so crowded I could hardly see across the room.

Ginny yelped as a snake began to crawl up her leg. "Let's get out of here!" she cried.

She yanked open the attic door. She and Foz hurried downstairs. I grabbed the magic case and followed them. A snake slithered after me.

"Get back in there!" I yelled. I picked up the snake and threw it into the attic room. I shut the door. I pushed on it to make sure it was closed. Then I ran downstairs and out to the back garden.

A gust of March wind slapped my face. Ginny's long hair flew out behind her.

"Snakes—yuck!" she squealed. "Tim—what are we going to do? When Mum and Dad see the attic, we're dead meat!"

Foz stared at the magic case. "What did you bring that out for? It's dangerous!"

"It's okay if we stay outside," I told him. "So what if a bunch of birds comes out? They'll fly away."

I wasn't as sure about that as I sounded. But I couldn't give Amaz-O's case back without seeing everything in it first. I just couldn't.

"Hurry up, Tim," Ginny whined. "I'm starving. It's lunchtime!"

"Wait. Wait." I opened the magic case. *Kaboom!* It didn't sound so loud outside— especially with the wind blowing as hard as it was.

I held the magic wand poised between my fingers. What does this thing do? I wondered.

I waved it around, trying out new magician names. "The Great Incredible-O. Mister Terrifico—that's not bad. Get out of there, Ginny!" She was rummaging through the magic kit.

"You promised we'd share it, remember?" she snapped. Then her face brightened. "Hey! Great!" She pulled a carrot out of Amaz-O's bag. "Just what I needed—something to eat."

"Put that back!" I ordered.

"It's still fresh," she said. "Yum!"

She opened her mouth, ready to bite the carrot.

"Ginny—no!" I cried. "Maybe you shouldn't eat that. Maybe—"

Ginny never listens to me.

She crunched down on the carrot.

A flash of white light blinded me for a moment.

When my eyes focused, I saw the most amazing thing I'd ever seen in my life!

The carrot dropped to the grass. Ginny's nose twitched. Then she began to shrink.

As she shrank, her hair turned from blonde to white. Her nose turned pink. White fur and whiskers sprouted from her face. She grew smaller, furrier, whiter. . .

"I don't believe it!" Foz gasped. "Your sister— she's a rabbit!"

Ginny sat on the grass, twitching her little pink nose. She stared at me with her rabbity eyes. She waved her little paws and made angry, rabbity noises.

"Man, she is *steamed*!" Foz cried.

I was stunned. "I wished it," I murmured. "And now it's come true."

"What are you talking about?" Foz demanded. He grabbed me by the shoulders. "Get it together, Tim. We've got to do something! What's going to happen when your parents get home?"

"I told Ginny I'd turn her into a rabbit," I explained, still dazed. "To get back at her for ruining all my magic shows. And now she *is* a rabbit!"

Ginny the rabbit rose on her hind legs, gesturing angrily at me. Then she bounced up and thumped my shin with one of her big rabbit feet.

"Ow!" I cried. "That hurts as much as one of her karate kicks!"

"Look in the kit, Tim," Foz urged me. "There's got to be some way to change her back."

"You're right. There's got to be!" My eyes fell on the carrot in the grass. "The carrot," I said. "When Ginny bit it, she turned into a rabbit. But maybe if a rabbit bites it, it turns into a girl!"

Foz shook his head. "Huh?"

I snatched up the carrot. "We've got to try it. There's nothing to lose, right? She's already a rabbit. What else could happen to her?"

I shoved the end of the carrot towards Ginny's mouth. "Come on, Ginny. Take another bite."

She stared at the carrot suspiciously. She clamped her mouth shut and turned her face away.

"You little brat!" I shouted. "You *want* me to get in trouble, don't you! You want to stay a rabbit just to get me in trouble!"

Foz grabbed the carrot out of my hand. "Calm down, Tim. You're scaring her!"

221

Ginny's long rabbit ears perked up—she heard something. I heard it, too. A car coming. Pulling into the driveway!

"Hurry, Ginny!" I cried. "I think Mum and Dad are home. Take a bite of the carrot. It'll turn you back into a girl. I know it will!"

Ginny eyed me suspiciously. She sniffed the carrot with her twitchy pink nose.

"Hurry!" I shouted again.

She opened her mouth and took a nibble of carrot.

Foz and I watched her in a panic. "Please let it work," I prayed. "Please let it work!"

Ginny's rabbit nose twitched. Her ears stood straight up. Then they flopped down.

Nothing happened. She was still a rabbit.

"Mum and Dad!" I cried. "They're here! Foz—stay with Ginny. If Mum and Dad ask, say she's your sister's rabbit!"

I ran to the driveway. A car was backing out—not Mum and Dad. Just somebody turning around in our driveway.

Phew. Close one.

The wind gusted as I ran back to Foz and Ginny. Foz was on his knees, digging through the magic kit. Ginny hopped up and down impatiently.

The magic wand lay in the grass. Maybe this will work now, I hoped, picking it up. I've got to change her back!

I waved the wand over Ginny. "Turn my sister back into a girl!" I cried.

Nothing.

"Maybe you need to say the spell in a rhyme," Foz suggested. "Magicians always do that."

"Okay." I waved the wand again. "Let me think . . . Magic wand, winds that whirl, turn Ginny back into a girl!"

The wand began to shake. "Something's happening!" I shouted.

The white tip of the wand broke open. Out popped a white silk handkerchief.

"Wow!" Foz gasped. A blue one flew out, then a red one, then a yellow one. The wind blew them away before I could catch them.

I turned back to Ginny. Still a rabbit.

"It didn't work," I said unhappily. I tossed the wand into the grass. "It only makes stupid handkerchiefs."

I crossed over to the magic case. Ginny leaped at me, trying to bite my leg.

"Watch out!" I warned her. "I'm trying to help you!"

She twitched her nose in disgust.

Foz moved aside as I dived into the magic kit. I dumped everything out. A slip of paper tumbled out of a pocket in the case.

I snatched it up. At the top of the paper I saw the word INSTRUCTIONS.

"Look!" I cried. "Instructions!" I patted Ginny between the ears. "I'll have you back to normal in a second."

I raised the paper to read what it said.

"'Instructions. To use the magic top hat . . .' No. That's not what I need right now. . ."

"Hurry, Tim!" Foz said.

I scanned the paper, searching for anything about rabbits. "Here's something!" I announced. "'The magic carrot. . .'"

Just then a strong gust of wind blasted across the garden. The paper flew out of my hands.

"No!" I shouted, grasping for the paper. "I need that!" I watched helplessly as it flew out of my reach—high up into the sky.

"Get that paper!" I screamed. The wind blew it across the garden. I darted after it.

Foz zoomed ahead of me, yelling, "I've got it! I've got it!" The paper floated within his reach. He dived for it.

Whoosh! Another strong gust of wind. The paper fluttered away. Foz fell flat on his face.

I ran past him, following the paper. It blew across my neighbour's garden.

"Get it!" Foz shouted, racing after me. "It's headed for the woods!"

The wind died for a minute. The paper settled on the grass.

I pounced on it. But the wind picked up before I landed. The paper blew away again.

"Rats!" I cried.

"There it goes!" Foz shouted. The paper drifted towards the stream.

The paper floated above the stream, then

landed in the water. Foz zipped across the garden to grab it.

"Don't let it get wet!" I screamed.

Too late. The paper was soaked.

"I've got it!" Foz shouted. He leaned over the stream and snatched at the paper. But the current carried it away.

Foz and I chased it down the stream, panting. But we couldn't run as fast as the current.

"It's getting away," I huffed. A few seconds later we lost sight of it.

Foz and I collapsed on the ground.

"That's it," I groaned. "We'll never get it back now. So how do I turn Ginny back into a girl?"

Foz heaved himself to his feet and pulled me up by the hand. "Don't panic, Tim. Panicking isn't going to help."

Great advice.

We hurried back to Ginny. I hoped maybe she'd magically turned back into a girl while we were gone. No such luck.

Ginny knew we hadn't found the instructions. She bounced around the garden, squealing angry rabbit squeals.

Foz rubbed his short hair as he watched her. "Boy, she's really stressed," he said.

I fell to my knees to talk to her. "Don't worry, Ginny," I soothed. "I've got an idea. I'm going to take you to Amaz-O right now. He'll turn you back into a girl. I'm sure he will."

With one of her long rabbit ears, Ginny flicked my nose. She couldn't say "Boi-oi-oing." She didn't have to. I knew what she meant.

"Let's pick this stuff up," I said to Foz. We began to gather all the tricks off the grass and pile them into Amaz-O's magic case. "Amaz-O won't want to help us if I don't give him back his magic kit."

Foz took my bike, balancing the magic kit on the handlebars. I picked up Ginny. "Come on, little rabbit sister," I cooed. She let me pull her up by the back—then nipped me on the wrist!

"Ow!" I dropped her. "Do you want me to help you or not?"

She hopped up and down angrily. I knew what she was thinking. If I didn't change her back into a girl, I'd be in as much trouble as she was. I had no choice.

I reached for her again. "Don't bite me this time," I warned her. "Or I'll put a muzzle over that little snout of yours."

She squirmed in my arms but didn't bite. I set her in the basket on her bike.

"To Midnight Mansion," I told Foz. We set off, pedalling hard against the strong wind.

I rode through town in a daze. Ginny's long white ears waved in my face.

Amaz-O's words rang in my ears. "Beat it, punk!" he'd said. I wondered if he'd really help me.

He's got to, I told myself. He'll be glad to get his magic kit back.

I'll make him help, I decided. I won't give him the kit until he turns Ginny back into a girl.

We pulled into the car park in front of Midnight Mansion. The old castle looked just as scary in the daytime as it did at night. There were no floodlights casting shadows on the stone towers. But the grey, vine-covered walls gave the place a spooky, abandoned feeling.

I skidded to a stop in front of the mansion. Foz carried the magic kit. I grabbed Ginny out of the bike basket.

"Behave," I warned her as we climbed the front steps to the mansion. "Remember, I'm trying to help you. Don't go biting me or anything."

She twitched her nose at me. She lifted her little rabbit lips and bared her tiny rabbit teeth.

"Go ahead—bite me," I whispered. "See how you like spending the rest of your life as a rabbit. You don't even *like* lettuce!"

She closed her mouth and twitched her nose again. It doesn't matter whether she's a girl or a rabbit, I thought. Either way she's a pain in the neck.

We stopped at the top of the steps.

"Oh, no!" I gasped. "I don't believe it!"

The sign on the front door read SORRY, WE'RE CLOSED.

"No!" I cried. I banged my forehead against the door.

Foz said, "This place gives me the creeps. It looks like Count Dracula's castle." He shivered. "Let's get out of here."

He set the magic case down. "Amaz-O's magic kit is so heavy. Do you think we can leave it by the door?"

I glared at him. "*No*, we can't leave it by the door. And we're not going home. Not yet."

I squeezed Ginny in my arms, thinking. "Okay, so the place is closed. But Amaz-O could be in there, rehearsing or something. Right?"

"He could be, I guess," Foz said. "But chances are—"

"We've got to take that chance," I insisted. I tried the front door. Locked. Of course.

"There must be another way in," I said. "A back door or something." I dashed down the steps and around the side of the club.

"Bring the case, Foz!" I ordered.

He followed me, lugging the kit. I kept my eyes peeled for guards.

At the back of the mansion we found a door. I tried it. It opened easily!

We crept inside. We found ourselves in the club's kitchen. It was long, narrow, and shiny clean. The lights were off, but we could see by the light from a window at one end.

Foz paused in front of a huge, stainless steel refrigerator. "I'll bet they've got some great food in here," he whispered. "Lemon meringue pie or something."

I tugged at his arm. "This is no time for a snack!" I snapped. "Come on!"

We left the kitchen and entered a long, dark hallway. I recognized that hall. It was the same hallway I'd walked down after my escape from the basement—the *first* time Amaz-O let me down.

"There'd better not be a second time," I muttered under my breath.

We tiptoed down the dark hall. Up ahead I saw the door to Amaz-O's dressing room. It was half-open. A dim light spilled out into the hallway.

Yes! I thought to myself. That's a good sign.

With Ginny in my arms, I crept up to the door. Please, please let him be in there, I prayed. Please be here, Amaz-O. Please help us.

I stopped in front of the door. I took a deep
breath.

"Mr Amaz-O? Are you here?"

No reply.

I tried again. "Mr Amaz-O? Hello?"

"He's not here," Foz said. "Let's go."

"Shhh!" I pushed the door open and crept into the dressing room. One small lamp cast a dim pool of light on the dressing table. The great Amaz-O sat on the couch, his left side facing the door. He was staring at the wall. He didn't seem to notice us.

"Mr Amaz-O?" I said politely. "It's me again. The kid you made disappear in your magic show."

I thought Amaz-O would turn his head to face us now, but he didn't. He didn't do anything. He just sat there.

Man, I thought. He really hates kids. Or he hates his fans. Or he hates all people. Or something.

When I become a great magician, I vowed, I won't be like Amaz-O. I won't let my fame go to my head. I'll be nice to people. This is ridiculous.

I didn't care what Amaz-O's problem was. I needed his help—badly. And I wouldn't give up until I got it.

I stepped further into the dressing room. "Mr Amaz-O, I'm sorry to bother you. But I really need your help. It's important."

Amaz-O didn't move. He stared at the wall. Silent.

"Do you think he's asleep?" Foz whispered.

I shrugged. I took another breath and crept closer to the couch.

"I know you told me to beat it," I said. "I wouldn't bother you if it wasn't a matter of life and death—I swear."

Still no response. I turned back to Foz, who cowered in the doorway. He looked as if he were ready to run for it. I waved him into the room.

Foz stepped in. He set the magic kit on the floor, shaking.

I stared at Amaz-O. He ignored me. Who does he think he is? I thought angrily. He can't treat me this way! I'm not leaving until he helps me turn Ginny back into a girl.

I steeled myself and approached the magician. He didn't look at me. I tapped him on the shoulder.

He toppled over on to his side. *Thunk!*

Foz gasped. "Is he—? Is he—?"

I peered at the body on the couch. "He isn't alive!" I cried. "Amaz-O isn't alive!"

"Oh, no!" Foz was wringing his hands in terror. "Oh, no! He's dead! He's dead! Help!"

"He's not dead," I said. "He's a dummy!"

"Amaz-O is nothing but a big wooden puppet!"

How could it be possible? I stared at the puppet on the couch. I couldn't resist touching its cheek—then pinching it—just to be sure.

Oh, wow!

It was true. Amaz-O was made of wood.

Foz sputtered, "But—I saw him on TV. He looked totally real."

"And I saw him live," I said. "On stage. I stood right next to him, and he made me disappear!"

How can this be? I wondered. How can the greatest magician in the world be a puppet?

"This can't be the guy you saw," Foz insisted, poking at the dummy. "This is probably just a dummy he keeps around for fun. The real Amaz-O has got to be around here somewhere."

Rabbit Ginny squirmed angrily in my arms. "Calm down," I ordered, trying to pet her.

She growled. I've never heard of a rabbit growling before. Only a Ginny-rabbit would growl.

Amaz-O, my idol, I thought bitterly. What a fake he turned out to be. Not only was he a jerk to me—he's not even a real person! He's a puppet!

"What are we going to do?" Foz asked.

I shook my head. I had no idea. "Now I'll never get Ginny changed back into a girl," I said. "Mum and Dad are going to *murder* me."

"Why don't you tell them she ran away?" Foz suggested. "They'll never believe you turned her into a rabbit, anyway."

"Why would she run away?" I demanded. "She was their little darling. She could do no wrong. *I'm* the one who should run away."

Foz lifted the Amaz-O puppet's head, studying it. "I wonder how this thing works..." he said.

A low voice suddenly growled, "Hey, punk—I told you to beat it!"

I froze. "Did you say something, Foz?" I asked.

He shook his head, eyes wide. He'd heard the voice, too.

"So beat it! Get out of here!" the voice growled.

I glanced around the room. I didn't see anyone.

"Did the puppet talk?" I asked Foz.

"I—I don't think so," he stammered. "The voice came from the other side of the room."

"The puppet didn't talk, dummy," the voice grumbled. I turned to find it. I gazed across the room. Amaz-O's white rabbit sat on a chair in front of the dressing table.

"I told you to get lost. Now get lost!" the rabbit growled.

"Tim—did—did you see that?" Foz stammered. "I think that rabbit talked."

"Of course I talked, stupid," the rabbit snarled.

"You talked?" I echoed in amazement.

"I guess that thing on the couch isn't the only dummy in this room," the rabbit snapped. "I can do lots of things. I'm a magician."

Foz and I stared at the rabbit, stunned. Even Ginny stopped squirming in my arms.

"You're not a magician," Foz said. "You're a rabbit."

The rabbit's ears twisted. "Duh. You guys are really quick. You know that?"

"You don't have to be so mean," I protested.

"*You* don't have to be so stupid," the rabbit replied. "I may *look* like a rabbit. But so does your little sister. Am I right?"

"He's got a point," Foz admitted.

"I am the great Amaz-O," the rabbit announced. "In person. That dummy on the couch is a puppet I had built to look like me—the old me."

My jaw fell open. "*You're* Amaz-O? What happened to you?"

The rabbit sighed. "It's a long story. Let's just

say I had a rival—a real powerful one. A sorcerer, actually."

Foz gasped. "A sorcerer? Do they really exist?"

"I'm telling you about one, aren't I?" the rabbit shouted.

"Yes, but—"

"So be quiet and listen to the story," Amaz-O, the rabbit, grumbled. "If you'd stop talking you might learn something."

Amaz-O sure was a grouch.

"Anyway, long story short," Amaz-O went on. "This sorcerer guy—Frank—"

"A sorcerer named Frank?" I cut in. I didn't mean to interrupt. It just slipped out.

The rabbit glared at me. "*Yes*, a sorcerer named Frank. You got a problem with that?"

I shook my head.

"Can I finish talking now? You got any more stupid questions?"

Foz and I both shook our heads.

"This guy's named Foz—" Amaz-O gestured towards Foz "—and you want to make fun of a guy named Frank."

"I'm sorry," I said. "I didn't mean to make fun of Frank."

"He's a very powerful guy," Amaz-O said. "I'm proof of that."

The rabbit hopped out of the chair, crossed the dressing room, and sat on the couch next to the dummy.

"Here's what happened," he began. "I was at the height of my fame. I was the most brilliant magician in the world. I made appearances on all the top TV shows. I had millions of fans. Dopey little kids like you looked up to me."

"Hey!" I protested. "Stop calling us dopey."

Amaz-O ignored me. He continued, "My tricks were the most amazing anyone had ever seen. And Frank was jealous. He was a sorcerer, working alone in a basement. He could cast amazing spells—but he was kind of ugly, with a high-pitched voice. People didn't take him seriously.

"He wanted to be famous like me, but he wasn't. So he turned me into a rabbit. Very funny, right? Ha ha. Turn the magician into a rabbit. Yuk, yuk, yuk."

Foz and I exchanged baffled glances. Amaz-O was turning out to be a little weird.

"I'm not powerful enough to reverse Frank's spell," Amaz-O went on. "I'm a magician, not a sorcerer. But I refused to let him stop me. So I built that mechanical dummy over there. I made him look just like me. And I kept on doing my shows, just as before."

"So you control the puppet?" Foz asked. "You make it look as if he's the magician, performing all the tricks?"

"I just said that, didn't I?" Amaz-O snapped. "Are you hard-of-hearing, kid?"

"You're really rude, you know that, Amaz-O?" I said. I was getting sick of his put-downs. "You're the rudest person—or rabbit, or whatever—I ever met in my life!"

Amaz-O's long ears drooped. "Hey—I'm sorry," he said. "Being a rabbit gets on my nerves. But also, I can't let people get too close— you know? I don't want anyone to find out my secret. It could ruin me."

Ginny squirmed in my arms again. I'd nearly forgotten all about her. I realized I'd better hurry up and ask Amaz-O to help me change her back.

"We're in terrible trouble, Amaz-O," I said, holding Ginny towards him. "This is my sister, Ginny. She ate some of the carrot that was in your magic kit—"

"So you confess, do you? You stole my magic kit!"

"I—I only borrowed it," I stammered. "I brought it back—see? I'm sorry."

"I'll bet you are," Amaz-O snapped.

"Can you help us, Amaz-O?" I pleaded. "Please, can you help me turn Ginny back into a girl?"

Amaz-O studied Ginny with his beady rabbit eyes. I held my breath waiting for his answer.

He settled deeper into the couch and shook his head. "Sorry," he said. "There's nothing I can do for her."

"Noooo!" I moaned, sinking into a chair. "You were my last chance. I'm doomed!"

"You didn't let me finish," Amaz-O said. "There's nothing I can do for her—because the magic will wear off by itself."

"Yo! All right!" Foz exclaimed happily. He shot both fists into the air.

"But when?" I asked. "My parents are coming home soon."

"How many bites of the carrot did she eat?" Amaz-O asked.

"Two," I replied.

"How long ago?"

"About an hour ago," I answered.

"Okay," Amaz-O said. "She should turn back into a girl in half an hour. Do you feel better now?"

I nodded and sighed with relief. That was a close one, I thought. But everything is going to be okay.

"Hey—" Foz said, jumping up. "We'd better hurry up and take Ginny home—before she turns back into a girl. We don't have enough bikes to go round!"

I pushed Ginny into his arms. "Take her home, Foz," I said. "I'll be there in a few minutes." I wanted to talk to Amaz-O a little longer.

Clutching Ginny in his arms, Foz hurried out of the dressing room. "Don't stay too long," he called over his shoulder. "I don't want to be alone with Ginny when she turns back into a girl. I have a feeling she's going to be in the mood to karate-chop somebody!"

In reply, Ginny beat her hind legs against his chest.

"I'm right behind you," I promised. Foz disappeared down the dark hallway.

"Listen, Amaz-O," I said. "I'm really sorry I stole your magic bag. I know it was a terrible thing to do."

"Shove this stupid dummy aside and sit down on the couch," Amaz-O said. I moved the dummy and sat down next to Amaz-O.

"You really love magic, don't you?" he said.

My heart started pounding. This was the heart-to-heart magician talk I'd been hoping to have with Amaz-O all along!

"It's my dream to be a magician," I told him.

243

"A great magician like you. I'd do anything. Anything!"

"Well, you were great in the show the other night," Amaz-O said. "You disappeared very well, kid."

"Thanks."

Amaz-O sat quietly for a moment. He seemed to be thinking.

"Say, kid—" he said at last. "How would you like to join the act? I'm getting really tired of working with that big wooden dummy over there."

"Me?" Now my heart was really racing. "You want me to join the act?" I got so excited I jumped off the couch. Then I quickly sat down again. "Do you mean it, Amaz-O? Do you think I could?"

Amaz-O hopped over to the dressing room door. He kicked it shut.

"Why don't we give you a try..."

And that's how I joined Amaz-O's act. I was so excited about being a magician, I said yes without even thinking about it. I guess I should've asked a few questions first.

Don't get me wrong. I love being on stage in front of clapping, cheering audiences.

But I don't like hiding inside the black top hat. And I hate it when the Amaz-O dummy pulls me up too hard by the ears. That really hurts.

I also hate it when they forget to clean my cage. Sometimes they forget about it for days!

I guess I made a little mistake. See, when Amaz-O said he was tired of working with the big dummy, I thought he wanted me to take the dummy's place.

I didn't realize he wanted to retire—and have me take *his* place!

I'm not complaining. Amaz-O gives me plenty

of juicy lettuce and all the carrots I can eat. I even have a stage name of my own now. At last. It may not be my first choice, but it's still a professional name—"Fluffy".

The best part is, I'm on stage every night in a real magic act! My dream—my all-time dream!

How many kids—er—I mean, rabbits—can say their all-time dream came true at age twelve?

I'm really lucky—don't you agree?

Goosebumps

Egg Monsters
From Mars

My sister, Brandy, asked for an egg hunt for her tenth birthday party. And Brandy always gets what she wants.

She flashes her smile, the one that makes the dimples pop up on her cheeks. And she puts on her little baby face. Opens her green eyes wide and tugs at her curly red hair. "Please? Please? Can I have an egg hunt at my party?"

There's no way Mum and Dad can ever say no to her.

If Brandy asked for a red, white and blue ostrich for her birthday, Dad would be out in the garage right now, painting an ostrich.

Brandy is good at getting her own way. Really good. I'm her older brother, Dana Johnson. And I admit it. Even I have trouble saying no to Brandy.

I'm not little and cute like my sister. I have straight black hair that falls over my forehead.

And I wear glasses. And I'm a little chubby. "Dana, don't look so serious." That's what Mum is always telling me.

"Dana has an old soul," Grandma Evelyn always says.

I don't really know what that means. I suppose she means I'm more serious than most twelve-year-olds.

Maybe that's true. I'm not really serious all the time. I'm just curious about a lot of things. I'm very interested in science. I like studying insects and plants and animals. I have an ant farm in my room. And two tarantulas.

And I have my own microscope. Last night I studied a toenail under the microscope. It was a lot more interesting than you might think.

I want to be a research scientist when I'm older. I'll have my own lab, and I'll study anything I want to.

Dad is a kind of chemist. He works for a perfume company. He mixes things together to make new smells. He calls them *fragrances*.

Before Mum met Dad, she worked in a lab. She did things with white rats.

So both of my parents are happy that I'm into science. They encourage me. But that doesn't mean they give me whatever I ask for.

If I asked Dad for a red, white and blue ostrich for my birthday, do you know what he'd say? He'd say, "Go and play with your sister's!"

Anyway, Brandy asked for an egg hunt for her birthday. Her birthday is a week before Easter, so it wasn't a crazy idea.

We have a very large back garden. It stretches all the way back to a small, trickling creek.

The garden is filled with bushes and trees and flower beds. And there's a big old kennel, even though we don't have a dog.

Lots of good egg-hiding places.

So Brandy got her egg hunt. She invited her entire class.

You may not think that egg hunts are exciting. But Brandy's was.

Brandy's birthday came on a warm and sunny day. Only a few small cumulus clouds high in the sky. (I study clouds.)

Mum hurried out to the back garden after breakfast, lugging a big bucket of eggs. "I'll help you hide them," I told her.

"That wouldn't be fair, Dana," Mum replied. "You're going to be in the egg hunt too—remember?"

I'd almost forgotten. Brandy usually doesn't want me hanging around when her friends come over. But today she said that I could be in the egg hunt. And so could my best friend, Anne Gravel.

Anne lives in the house next door. My mum is best friends with Anne's mum. Mrs Gravel agreed to let Mum hide eggs all over their back garden too. So it's only fair that Anne gets to join in.

Anne is tall and skinny, and has long red-brown hair. She's nearly a head taller than me. So everyone thinks she's older. But she's twelve too.

Anne is very funny. She's always cracking jokes. She makes fun of me because I'm so serious. But I don't mind. I know she's only joking.

That afternoon Anne and I stood on the driveway and watched the kids from Brandy's class arrive at the party. Brandy handed each one of them a little straw basket.

They were really excited when Brandy told them about the egg hunt. And the girls got even more excited when Brandy told them the grand prize—one of those expensive American Girl dolls.

Of course the boys started to grumble. Brandy should have had a prize a boy might like. Some of the boys started using their baskets as Frisbees. And others began wrestling in the grass.

"I was a lot more sophisticated when I was ten," I muttered to Anne.

"When you were ten, you liked Ninja Turtles," Anne replied, rolling her eyes.

"I did not!" I protested.

"Yes, you did," Anne insisted. "You wore a Ninja Turtle T-shirt to school every day."

I kicked some gravel across the driveway. "Just because I wore the shirt doesn't mean I liked them," I replied.

Anne flung back her long hair. She sneered at me. I hate it when Anne sneers at me. "You had Ninja Turtle cups and plates at your tenth birthday party, Dana. And a Ninja Turtle tablecloth. And we played some kind of Ninja Turtle Pizza Pie-throwing game."

"But that doesn't mean I liked them!" I declared.

Three more girls from Brandy's class came running across the lawn. I recognized them. They were the girls I call the Hair Sisters. They're not sisters. But they spend all their time in Brandy's room after school doing each other's hair.

Dad moved slowly across the grass towards them. He had his camcorder up to his face. The three Hair Sisters waved to the camera and yelled, "Happy Birthday, Brandy!"

Dad tapes all our birthdays and holidays and big events. He keeps the tapes on a shelf in the playroom. We never watch them.

The sun beamed down. The grass smelled sweet and fresh. The spring leaves on the trees were just starting to unfurl.

"Okay—everyone follow me to the back!" Brandy ordered.

The kids lined up in twos and threes, carrying their baskets. Anne and I followed behind them.

Dad walked backwards, busily taping everything.

Brandy led the way to the back garden. Mum was waiting there. "The eggs are hidden everywhere," Mum announced, sweeping her hand in the air. "Everywhere you can imagine."

"Okay, everyone!" Brandy cried. "At the count of three, the egg hunt begins! *One*—"

Anne leaned down and whispered in my ear. "Bet you five dollars I collect more eggs than you."

I smiled. Anne always knows how to make things more interesting.

"*Two*—"

"You've got a bet!" I told her.

"*Three!*" Brandy called.

The kids all cheered. The hunt for hidden eggs was on.

They all began hurrying through the back garden, bending down to pick up eggs. Some of them moved on hands and knees through the grass. Some worked in groups. Some searched through the garden on their own.

I turned and saw Anne stooping down, moving quickly along the side of the garage. She already had three eggs in her basket.

I can't let her win! I told myself. I sprang into action.

I ran past a cluster of girls around the old kennel. And I kept moving.

I wanted to find an area of my own. A place where I could grab up a bunch of eggs without having to compete with the others.

I jogged across the tall grass, making my way to the back. I was all alone, nearly to the creek, when I started my search.

I spotted an egg hidden behind a small rock. I had to move fast. I wanted to win the bet.

I bent down, picked it up, and quickly dropped it into my basket.

Then I knelt down, set my basket on the ground, and started to search for more eggs.

But I jumped up when I heard a scream.

"Aaaaaiiiiii!"

The scream rang through the air.

I turned back towards the house. One of the Hair Sisters was waving her hand wildly, calling to the other girls. I grabbed up my basket and ran towards her.

"They're not hard-boiled!" I heard her cry as I came closer. And I saw the drippy yellow yolk running down the front of her white T-shirt.

"Mum didn't have time to hard-boil them," Brandy announced. "Or to paint them. I know it's weird. But there just wasn't time."

I raised my eyes to the house. Mum and Dad had both disappeared inside.

"Be careful," Brandy warned her party guests. "If you crack them—"

She didn't finish her sentence. I heard a wet *splat*.

Then laughter.

A boy had tossed an egg against the side of the kennel.

"Cool!" one of the girls exclaimed.

Anne's big sheepdog, Stubby, came running out of the kennel. I don't know why he likes to sleep in there. He's almost as big as the kennel.

But I didn't have time to think about Stubby.

Splat!

Another egg exploded, this time against the garage wall.

More laughter. Brandy's friends thought it was really hilarious.

"Egg fight! Egg fight!" two boys started to chant.

I ducked as an egg went sailing over my head. It landed with a *craaack* on the driveway.

Eggs were flying everywhere now. I stood there and gaped in amazement.

I heard a shrill shriek. I spun around to see that two of the Hair Sisters had runny yellow yolk oozing in their hair. They were shouting and tugging at their hair and trying to pull the yellow gunk off with both hands.

Splat! Another egg hit the garage.

Craaack! Eggs bounced over the driveway.

I ducked down and searched for Anne. She's probably gone home, I figured. Anne enjoys a good laugh. But she's twelve, much too sophisticated for a babyish egg fight.

Well, when I'm wrong, I'm wrong.

257

"Think fast, Dana!" Anne screamed from behind me. I threw myself to the ground just in time. She heaved two eggs at once. They both whirred over my head and dropped on to the grass with a sickening *crack*.

"Stop it! Stop it!" I heard Brandy shrieking desperately. "It's my birthday! Stop it! It's my birthday!"

Thunk! Somebody hit Brandy in the chest with an egg.

Wild laughter rang out. Sticky yellow puddles covered the back lawn.

I raised my eyes to Anne. She was grinning back at me, about to let me have it again.

Time for action. I reached into my basket and pulled out the one and only egg I had picked up.

I raised it high above my head. Started to throw—but stopped.

The egg.

I lowered it and stared at it.

Stared hard at it.

Something was wrong with the egg.

Something was terribly wrong.

The egg was too big. Bigger than a normal egg. About the size of a softball.

I held it carefully, studying it. The colour wasn't right either. It wasn't egg-coloured. That creamy off-white. And it wasn't brown.

The egg was pale green. I raised it to the sun-light to make sure I was seeing correctly.

Yes. Green.

And what were those thick cracks up and down the shell?

I ran my index finger over the dark, jagged lines.

No. Not cracks. Some kind of veins. Blue-and-purple veins criss-crossing the green eggshell.

"Weird!" I muttered out loud.

Brandy's friends were shouting and shrieking. Eggs were flying all around me. An egg splattered over my trainers. The yellow yolk oozed over my laces.

But I didn't care.

I rolled the strange egg over and over slowly between my hands. I brought it close to my face and squinted hard at the blue-and-purple veins.

"Ooh." I let out a cry when I felt it pulsing.

The veins throbbed. I could feel a steady beat. *Thud. Thud. Thud.*

"Oh wow. *It's alive!*" I cried.

What had I found? It was totally weird. I couldn't wait to get it to my worktable and examine it.

But first I had to show it to Anne.

"Anne! Hey—Anne!" I called and started jogging towards her, holding the egg high in both hands.

I was staring at the egg. So I didn't see Stubby, her big sheepdog, run in front of me.

"Whooooa!"

I let out a cry as I fell over the dog.

And landed with a sickening *crunch* on top of my egg.

I jumped up quickly. Stubby started to lick my face. That dog has the *worst* breath!

I shoved him away and bent down to examine my egg.

"Hey!" I cried out in amazement. The egg wasn't broken. I picked it up carefully and rolled it in my hands.

Not a crack.

What a tough shell! I thought. My chest had landed on top of the egg. Pushed it into the ground. But the shell hadn't broken.

I wrapped my hands around the big egg as if soothing it.

I could feel the blue-and-purple veins pulsing.

Is something inside getting ready to hatch? I wondered. What kind of bird was inside it? Not a chicken, I knew. This was definitely not a hen's egg.

Splat!

Another egg smacked the side of the garage.

Kids were wrestling in the runny puddles of yolk on the grass. I turned in time to see a boy crack an egg over another boy's head.

"Stop it! Stop it!"

Brandy was screaming at the top of her lungs, trying to stop the egg fight before every single egg was smashed. I turned and saw Mum and Dad running across the garden.

"Hey, Anne—!" I called. I climbed to my feet, holding the weird egg carefully. Anne was frantically tossing eggs at three girls. The girls were bombarding her. Three to one—but Anne wasn't retreating.

"Anne—check this out!" I called, hurrying over to her. "You won't believe this egg!"

I stepped up beside her and held the egg out to her.

"No! Wait—!" I cried.

Too late.

Anne grabbed my egg and heaved it at the three girls.

"No—stop!" I wailed.

As I stared in horror, one of the three girls caught the egg in mid-air—and tossed it back.

I dived for it, making a head-first slide. And grabbed the egg in one hand before it hit the gravel.

Was it broken?

No.

This shell must be made of steel! I told myself. I pulled myself to my feet, gripping the egg carefully. To my surprise, it felt hot. Burning hot.

"Whoa!" I nearly dropped it.

Throb. Throb. Throb.

It pulsed rapidly. I could feel the veins beating against my fingers.

I wanted to show the egg to Mum and Dad. But they were busy breaking up the egg fight.

Dad's face was bright red. He was shouting at Brandy and pointing to the yellow stains up and down the side of the garage.

263

Mum was trying to calm down two girls who were crying. They had egg yolk stuck to their hair and all over their clothes. They even had it stuck to their eyebrows. I guess that's why they were crying.

Behind them Stubby was having a feast. He was running around in circles, lapping up egg after egg from the grass, his bushy tail wagging like crazy.

What a party!

I decided to take my weird egg inside. I wanted to study it later. Maybe I'd break off a tiny piece of shell and look at it under the microscope. Then I'd make a tiny hole in the shell and try to see inside.

Throb. Throb.

The veins pounded against my hand. The egg still felt hot.

It might be a turtle egg, I decided. I walked carefully to the house, cradling it in both hands.

One morning last fall, Anne had found a big box turtle on the kerb in front of her house. She carried it into her back garden and called me over. She knew I'd want to study it.

It was a pretty big turtle. About the size of a lunch box. Anne and I wondered how it got to her kerb.

Up in my room I had a book about turtles. I knew the book would help me identify it. I had hurried home to get the book. But Mum wouldn't let me go back out. I had to stay inside and have lunch.

When I got back to Anne's back garden, the turtle had vanished. I guess it wandered away.

Turtles can be pretty fast when they want to be.

As I carried my treasure into the house, I thought it might be a turtle egg. But why was it so hot? And why did it have those yucky veins all over it?

Eggs don't have veins—do they?

I hid the egg in my dressing-table drawer. I surrounded it with my rolled socks to protect it. Then I closed the drawer slowly, carefully, and returned to the back garden.

Brandy's guests were all leaving as I stepped outside. They were covered in sticky eggs. They didn't look too happy.

Brandy didn't look too happy, either. Dad was busy shouting at her, angrily waving his arms, pointing to the gloppy egg stains all over the lawn.

"Why did you let this happen?" he screamed at her. "Why didn't you stop it?"

"I tried!" Brandy wailed. "I tried to stop it!"

"We'll have to have the garage painted," Mum murmured, shaking her head. "How will we ever mow the lawn?"

"This was the worst party I ever had!" Brandy cried. She bent down and pulled chunks of eggshell from her trainer laces. Then she glared up at Mum. "It's all *your* fault!"

"Huh?" Mum gasped. "My fault?"

"You didn't hard-boil the eggs," Brandy accused. "So it's all your fault."

Mum started to protest—but bit her lip instead.

Brandy stood up and tossed the bits of eggshell to the ground. She flashed Mum her best dimpled smile. "Next year for my birthday, can we have a Make Your Own Ice-Cream Sundae party?"

That evening I wanted to study my weird green egg. But we had to visit Grandma Evelyn and Grandpa Harry and take them out to dinner. They always make a big fuss about Brandy's birthday.

First, Brandy had to open her presents. Grandma Evelyn bought her a pair of pink fuzzy slippers that Brandy will never wear. She'll probably give them to Stubby as chew toys.

Brandy opened the biggest box next. She pulled out a pair of pink-and-white pyjamas. Brandy made a big fuss about them and said she really needed pyjamas. She did a pretty good acting job.

But how excited can you get over pyjamas?

Her last present was a twenty-five-dollar gift certificate for the CD store at the mall. Nice present. 'I'll go with you to make sure you don't pick out anything lame," I offered.

Brandy pretended she didn't hear me.

She gave our grandparents big hugs. Brandy is a big hugger. Then we all went out for dinner at the new Italian restaurant on the corner.

What did we talk about at dinner? Brandy's wild birthday party. When we told Grandma and Grandpa about the egg fight, they laughed and laughed.

It wasn't so funny in the afternoon. But a few hours later at dinner, we all had to admit it was pretty funny. Even Dad managed a smile or two.

I kept thinking about the egg in my dressing-table drawer. When we got back home, would I find a baby turtle on my socks?

Dinner stretched on and on. Grandpa Harry told all of his funny golfing stories. He tells them every time we visit. We always laugh anyway.

We didn't return home till really late. Brandy fell asleep in the car. And I could barely keep my eyes open.

I slunk up to my room and changed into pyjamas. Then, with a loud yawn, I turned off the light. I knew I'd fall asleep the moment my head hit the pillow.

I fluffed my pillow the way I liked it. Then I slid into bed and pulled the quilt up to my chin.

I started to settle my head on the pillow when I heard the sound.

Thump. Thump. Thump.

Steady like a heartbeat. Only louder.

Much louder.

THUMP. THUMP. THUMP.

So loud, I could hear the dressing-table drawers rattling.

I sat straight up. Wide awake now. I stared through the darkness to my dressing-table.

THUMP. THUMP. THUMP.

I turned and lowered my feet to the floor.

Should I open the drawer?

I sat in the darkness, trembling with excitement. With fear.

Listening to the steady thud.

Should I open the drawer and check it out?

Or should I run as far away as I could?

Thump, thump, THUMP.

I had to see what was happening in my dressing-table drawer.

Had the egg hatched? Was the turtle bumping up against the sides of the drawer, trying to climb out?

Was it a turtle?

Or was it something weird?

Suddenly I felt very afraid of it.

I took a deep breath and rose to my feet. My legs felt rubbery and weak as I made my way across the room. My mouth was suddenly as dry as cotton.

Thump, THUMP, thump.

I clicked on the light. Blinked several times, struggling to force my eyes to focus.

The steady thuds grew louder as I approached the dressing-table.

Heartbeats, I told myself.

Heartbeats of the creature inside the egg.

I grabbed the drawer handles with both hands. Took another deep breath.

Dana, this is your last chance to run away, I warned myself.

This is your last chance to leave the drawer safely closed.

Thump, thump, thump, thump, thump.

I tugged open the drawer and peered inside.

I stared in, amazed that nothing had changed. The egg sat exactly where I had left it. The blue-and-purple veins along the shell pulsed as before.

Feeling a little calmer, I picked it up.

"Ouch!"

I nearly dropped it. The shell was burning hot.

I cupped it in my hands and blew on it. "This is so totally weird," I murmured to myself.

Mum and Dad have to see it, I decided. Right now. Maybe they can tell me what it is.

They were still awake. I could hear them talking in their room down the hall.

I carried the egg carefully, cradling it in both hands. I had to knock on their door with my elbow. "It's me," I said.

"Dana, what is it?" Dad demanded grumpily. "It's been a long day. We're all very tired."

I pushed open their door a crack. "I have an egg I want to show you," I started.

"No eggs!" they both cried at once.

"Haven't we seen enough eggs for one day?" Mum griped.

"It's a very strange egg," I insisted. "I can't identify it. I think—"

"Good night, Dana," Dad interrupted.

"Please don't ever mention eggs again," Mum added. "Promise?"

"Well, I. . ." I stared down at the pulsing green egg in my hand. "It'll only take a second. If you'll just—"

"Dana!" Dad yelled. "Why don't you go sit on it and hatch it?"

"Clark—don't talk to Dana that way!" Mum scolded.

"He's twelve years old. He can take a joke," Dad protested.

They started arguing about how Dad should talk to me.

I muttered good night and started back to my room.

I mean, I can take a hint.

Thump. Thump. The egg pulsed in my hand.

I had a sudden impulse to crack it open and see what was inside. But of course I would never do that.

I stopped outside Brandy's room. I was desperate to show my weird treasure to somebody. I knocked on her door.

No answer.

271

I knocked again, a little harder. Brandy is a very heavy sleeper.

Still no answer.

I started to knock a third time—and the door flew open. Brandy greeted me with an open-mouthed yawn. "What's wrong? Why'd you wake me?"

"I want to show you this egg," I told her.

She narrowed her eyes at me. "You're serious? After what happened at my party? After the worst birthday party in the history of America, you really want to show me an egg?"

I held it up. "Yeah. Here it is."

She slammed the door in my face.

"You mean you don't want to see it?" I called in.

No reply.

Once again, I could take a hint. I carried the egg back to my room and set it down carefully in the dressing-table drawer. Then I closed the drawer and climbed back into bed.

Thump. Thump. Thump.

I fell asleep to the steady throbbing.

The next morning, I woke up just in time to watch the egg hatch.

A loud cracking sound woke me up.

Blinking, I pulled myself up on one elbow. Still half-asleep, I thought I heard Brandy cracking her knuckles.

That's one of Brandy's secret talents. She never does it when adults are around. But when you're alone, she can crack out entire symphonies on her knuckles.

Another loud crack snapped me alert.

The dressing-table. The noises were coming from my dressing-table.

I heard a long *rip*, like Velcro ripping open. Then more cracks. Like cracking bones.

And I knew it had to be the egg.

My heart started to pound. I leaped up. Grabbed my glasses and slapped them on to my face. My legs got tangled in the bedsheet, and I nearly went sprawling over the floor.

I hurtled across the room. The egg was hatching—and I had to be there in time to watch.

273

I grabbed the drawer handles and eagerly pulled the drawer open. I was so eager, I nearly pulled the drawer out of the table!

Catching my balance, I gripped the table top with both hands and stared down at the egg.

Craaaaack!

The blue-and-purple veins throbbed. A long, jagged crack split across the green shell.

Unh unh.

I heard a low grunt from inside the egg. The grunt of a creature working hard to push out.

Unnnnnh.

What a struggle!

It doesn't sound like a turtle, I told myself. Is it some kind of exotic bird? Like a parrot? Or a flamingo maybe?

How would a flamingo egg get in my back garden?

How would *any* weird egg get in my back garden?

Unnnh unnnnh.

Craaaaack!

The sounds were really gross.

I rubbed my eyes and squinted down at the egg. It was bouncing and bobbing in the drawer now. Each grunt made the egg move.

The veins throbbed. Another crack split along the front of the shell. And thick yellow goo poured out into the drawer, seeping on to my socks.

"Yuck!" I cried.

The egg shook. Another crack. More of the thick liquid oozed down the egg and on to my socks.

The egg bobbed and bounced. I heard more hard grunting. *Unnnnh. Unnnnh.* The egg trembled with each grunt.

Yellow slime oozed as the cracks in the shell grew wider. The veins pulsed. The egg shook.

And then a large triangle of shell broke off. It fell into the drawer.

I leaned closer to stare into the hole in the egg. I couldn't really see what was inside. I could see only wet yellow blobby stuff.

Unnh-unnnnnh.

Another grunt—and the eggshell crackled and fell apart. Yellow liquid spilled into the drawer, soaking my socks.

I held my breath as a weird creature pushed itself out of the breaking shell. A yellow, lumpy thing.

A baby chicken?

No way.

I couldn't see a head. Or wings. Or feet.

I gripped the dressing-table top and stared down at it. The strange animal pushed away the last section of shell. This was amazing!

It rolled wetly over my socks.

A blob. A sticky, shiny yellow blob.

It looked like a pile of very runny scrambled eggs.

Except it had tiny green veins criss-crossing all over it.

My chest felt about to explode. I finally remembered to breathe. I let out my breath in a long whoosh. My heart was thudding.

The yellow blob throbbed. It made sick, wet sucking sounds.

It turned slowly. And I saw round black eyes near its top.

No head. No face. Just two tiny black eyes on top of the lumpy yellow body.

"You're not a chicken," I murmured out loud. My voice came out in a choked whisper. "You're definitely not a chicken."

But what was it?

"Hey—Mum! Dad!" I shouted.

They had to see this creature. They had to see the scientific discovery of the century!

"Mum! Dad! Hurry!"

No response.

The lumpy creature stared up at me. Throbbing. Its tiny green veins pulsing. Its eggy body bouncing.

"Mum? Dad?"

Silence.

I stared into my drawer.

What should I do?

I had to show it to Mum and Dad. I carefully closed the drawer so it couldn't bounce out and escape. Then I went running downstairs, shouting at the top of my voice.

My pyjama trousers were twisted, and I nearly fell down the stairs. "Mum! Dad! Where *are* you?"

The house was silent. The vacuum cleaner had been pulled out of the closet. But no one was around to use it.

I burst into the kitchen. Were they still having breakfast?

"Mum? Dad? Brandy?"

No one there.

Sunlight streamed in through the kitchen window. The breakfast dishes—three cereal bowls and two coffee cups—were stacked beside the sink.

Where did they go? I wondered, my heart pounding. How could they leave when I had the most amazing thing in the history of the known universe to show them?

I turned to leave the kitchen when I saw the note on the fridge. It was written in blue ink in Mum's handwriting. I snatched it off the magnet and read it:

"Dad and I taking Brandy to her piano lesson. Get yourself some cereal. Love, M."

Cereal?

Cereal?

How could I think about cereal at a time like this?

What should I do now?

I leaned my forehead against the cool fridge, struggling to think. I couldn't leave the throbbing egg blob locked up in the drawer all morning. Maybe it needed fresh air. Maybe it needed exercise. Maybe it needed food.

Food? I swallowed hard. What would it eat? What *could* it eat? It was just a lump of scrambled eggs with eyes.

I've got to take it out of there, I decided. I've got to show it to someone.

I thought instantly of Anne.

"Yes!" I exclaimed to myself. I'll take it next door and show it to Anne. She has a dog. She's really good with pets and animals. Maybe she'll have some idea of what I should do with it.

I hurried back upstairs and pulled on the jeans and T-shirt I had tossed on the floor

278

the night before. Then I made my way to the dressing-table and slid open the drawer.

"Yuck!"

The egg blob sat in its own yellow slime. Its whole body throbbed. The tiny, round eyes stared up at me.

"I'm taking you to Anne's," I told it. "Maybe the two of us can figure out what you are."

Only one problem.

How do I take it there?

I rubbed my chin, staring down at it. Do I carry it on a plate? No. It might tumble off.

A bowl?

No. A jar?

No. It couldn't breathe.

A box.

Yes. I'll put it in a box, I decided. I opened my wardrobe, dropped to my hands and knees, and shuffled through all the junk piled on the floor.

That's how I clean my room. I toss everything into the wardrobe and shut the door. I have the cleanest room in the house. No problem.

The only problem is finding things in my wardrobe. If I'm searching for something to wear, sometimes it takes a few days.

Today I was lucky. I found what I was looking for straight away. It was a shoe box. The box my new trainers came in.

I picked up the shoe box from the clutter and climbed to my feet. Then I kicked a heap of stuff back into the wardrobe so I could get the door closed.

"Okay!" I cried happily. I returned to the throbbing egg glob. "I'm carrying you to Anne's in this box. Ready?"

I didn't expect it to answer. And it didn't.

I pulled off the shoe box lid and set it on the top of the dressing-table. Then I lowered the box to the drawer.

"Now what?" I asked myself out loud.

How do I get it in the box? Do I just pick it up?

Pick it up in my hand?

I held the box in my left hand and started to reach into the drawer with my right. But then I jerked my hand away.

Will it bite me? I wondered.

How can it? It doesn't have a mouth.

Will it sting me? Will it hurt me somehow?

My throat tightened. My hand started to tremble. It was so gross—so wet and eggy.

Pick it up, Dana, I told myself. Stop being such a wimp. You're a scientist—remember? You have to be bold. You have to be daring.

That's true, I knew. Scientists can't back away from something just because it's yucky and gross.

I took a deep breath.

I counted to three.

Then I reached for it.

As my hand moved towards it, the creature began to tremble. It shook like a glob of yellow jelly.

I pulled back once again.

I can't do it, I decided. I can't pick it up with my bare hands. It might be too dangerous.

I watched it shake and throb. Wet bubbles formed on its eggy skin.

Is it scared of me? I wondered. Or is it trying to warn me away?

I had to find something to pick it up with. I turned and glanced around the room. My eyes landed on my baseball glove tucked on the top shelf of my bookcase.

Maybe I could pick up the egg creature in the glove and drop it into the shoe box. I was half-way across the room when I decided I didn't want to get my glove all wet and gloppy.

I need to shovel it into the box, I thought.

A little shovel would make the job easy. I walked back to the dressing-table. The egg creature was still shaking like crazy. I closed the drawer. Maybe the darkness will calm it down, I thought.

I made my way down to the basement. Mum and Dad keep all their gardening supplies down there. I found a small metal trowel and carried it back up to my room.

When I pulled open the drawer, the eggy blob was still shaking. "Don't worry, fella," I told it. "I'm a scientist. I'll be really gentle."

I don't think it understands English. As I lowered the trowel into the drawer, the green veins on the throbbing body began to pulse.

The creature started bobbing up and down. The little black eyes bulged up at me. I had the feeling the little guy was about to explode or something.

"Easy. Easy," I whispered.

I lowered the trowel carefully beside it. Then I slowly, slowly slid it under the throbbing creature.

"There. Gotcha," I said softly.

It wiggled and shook on the blade of the trowel. I began to lift it carefully from the drawer.

The shoe box sat on top of the dressing-table. I had the trowel in my right hand. I reached for the shoe box with my left.

Up, up. Slowly. Very slowly, I raised the egg creature towards the box.

Up. Up.

Almost to the box.

And the creature *growled* at me!

A low, gruff growl—like an angry dog.

"Ohhh!" I uttered a startled cry—and the trowel dropped from my hand.

"Yaaiii!" I let out another cry as it clanged across the floor—and the egg creature plopped wetly on to my trainer.

"No!"

Without thinking, I bent down and grabbed it up in my hand.

I'm holding it! I realized, my heart pounding.

I'm holding it.

What's going to happen to me?

Nothing happened.

No shock jolted my body. No rash spread instantly over my skin. My hand didn't fall off.

The creature felt warm and soft, like runny scrambled eggs.

I realized I was squeezing it tightly. Too tightly? I loosened my grip.

And lowered it into the shoe box. And fastened the lid over the top.

I set the shoe box down on the top of the dressing-table and examined my hand. It felt wet and sticky. But the skin hadn't turned yellow or peeled off or anything.

I could hear the creature pulsing inside the box.

"Don't growl like that again," I told it. "You scared me."

I grabbed some tissues and wiped off my hand. I kept my eyes on the box. The creature was bouncing around in there.

What kind of animal is it? I wondered.

I wished Mum and Dad were home. I really, really wanted to show it to them.

I glanced at the clock radio on my bedside table. Only nine o'clock. Anne might still be sleeping. Sometimes she sleeps until noon on Saturdays. I'm not really sure why. She says it makes the day go faster. Anne is a pretty weird girl.

I lifted the box with both hands. The egg creature felt surprisingly heavy. I made sure the lid was on tight. Then I carried it down the stairs and out the back door.

It was a sunny, warm day. A soft breeze made the fresh spring leaves tremble on the trees. Two houses down Mr Simpson was already mowing his back lawn. Near the garage two robins were having a tug-of-war over a fat brown earthworm.

I carried the box to Anne's back door. The door was open. I peered through the screen.

"Hi, Dana. Come in," Anne's mother called from in front of the sink.

Balancing the box against my chest, I pulled open the screen door and stepped into the kitchen. Anne sat at the breakfast table. She wore a big blue T-shirt over black cycling shorts. Her red-brown hair was tied behind her head in a long ponytail.

Three guesses what she was eating for breakfast.

You got it. Scrambled eggs.

"Yo, Dana!" she greeted me. "What's up?"

"Well—"

Mrs Gravel moved to the stove. "Dana, have you had breakfast? Can I make you some scrambled eggs?"

My stomach churned. I swallowed hard. "No. I don't think so."

"Nice fresh eggs," Mrs Gravel insisted. "I could make them fried if you don't like scrambled."

"No thanks," I replied weakly.

I felt the eggy blob bounce inside the box.

"I might need some more," Anne told her mum, shovelling in a big glob. "These eggs are great, Mum."

Mrs Gravel cracked an egg on the side of the frying-pan. "Maybe I'll make one for myself," she said.

All this egg talk was making me sick.

Anne finished her orange juice. "Hey—what's in the box? New trainers?"

"Uh . . . no," I replied. "Check this out, Anne. You won't believe what I found."

I was so eager to show it to her! Holding the box in front of me with both hands, I started across the kitchen.

And tripped over Stubby.

Again!

That big dumb sheepdog always got underfoot.

"Whooooaaa!" I let out a cry as I fell over the dog—and watched the shoe box fly into the air.

I landed on top of Stubby and got a mouthful of fur.

I struggled frantically to my feet.

And saw the egg creature sail out of the box and drop on to Anne's breakfast plate.

Anne's mouth dropped open. Her face twisted in disgust. "Oh, yuck!" she wailed. "Rotten eggs! Gross! Rotten eggs!"

"No—it's alive!" I protested.

But I don't think anyone heard me. Stubby jumped up on me as I started to explain, and nearly knocked me down again.

"Down, boy! Down!" Mrs Gravel scolded. "You know better than that."

"Get this away!" Anne demanded, shoving her plate across the table.

Her mum examined the plate, then glared at me. "Dana, what's wrong with you? This isn't funny. You ruined perfectly good scrambled eggs."

"You spoiled my breakfast!" Anne cried angrily.

"No, wait—" I protested.

But I wasn't fast enough.

Mrs Gravel grabbed up the plate. She carried

it to the sink, clicked on the garbage disposal—
and started to empty the egg creature into the
roaring drain.

"Nooooo!"

I let out a shriek—and dived for the sink.

I made a wild grab and pulled the creature from the drain.

No. I pulled a handful of *scrambled eggs* from the drain!

The egg creature rolled around the sink and started to slide towards the gurgling drain. I tossed the scrambled eggs down and grabbed the creature as it started to drop towards the grinding blades.

The lumpy yellow blob felt hot in my hands. I could feel the veins throbbing. The whole creature pulsed rapidly, like a racing heart.

I raised it up to my face and examined it. Still in one piece. "I saved your life!" I told it. "Phew! What a close one!"

I balanced it carefully in my palm. It shuddered and throbbed. Wet bubbles rolled down its lumpy sides. The black eyes stared up at me.

289

"What *is* that thing?" Anne demanded, getting up from the breakfast table. She straightened her long ponytail. "Is it a puppet? Did you make it out of an old sock or something?"

Before I could answer, Mrs Gravel gave me a gentle push towards the kitchen door. "Get it out of here, Dana," she ordered. "It's disgusting." She pointed down. "Look. It's dripping some kind of eggy goo all over my kitchen floor."

"I—I found it out the back," I started. "I don't really know what it is, but—"

"Out," Anne's mum insisted. She held open the screen door for me. "Out. I mean it. I don't want to have to wash the whole floor."

I didn't have a choice. I carried the egg creature out into the back garden. It seemed a little calmer. At least it wasn't trembling and pulsing so hard.

Anne followed me to the driveway. The bright sun made the egg creature gleam. My hands felt slimy and wet. I didn't want to squeeze it too tightly. But I also didn't want to let it fall.

"Is it a puppet?" Anne demanded. She bent down to see it better. "Yuck. It's alive?"

I nodded. "I don't know what it is. But it's definitely alive. I found it yesterday. At Brandy's party."

Anne continued to study the yellow blob. "You found it? Where?"

"I found an egg back by the creek," I told her. "A very weird-looking egg. I took it home, and it hatched this morning. And this is what came out."

"But what *is* it?" Anne asked. She gingerly poked its side with an index finger. "Oh, yuck. It's wet and mushy."

"It's not a chicken," I replied.

"Really," Anne said, rolling her eyes. "Did you figure that out all by yourself?"

"I thought it might be a turtle egg," I said, ignoring her sarcasm.

She squinted harder at it. "Do you think it's a turtle without its shell? Do turtles hatch without their shells?"

"I don't think so," I replied.

"Maybe it's some kind of mistake," Anne suggested. "A freak of nature. You know. Like you!" She laughed.

Anne has a great sense of humour.

She poked the egg creature again. The creature let out a soft wheeze of air. "Maybe you discovered a new species," Anne suggested. "A whole new kind of animal that's never been seen before."

"Maybe," I replied. That was an exciting idea.

"They'll name it after you," Anne teased. "They'll call it the Dodo!" She laughed again.

"You're not being very helpful," I said sharply. And then I had an idea.

"Know what I'm going to do with it?" I said, cupping it carefully between my hands. "I'm going to take it to that little science lab."

She narrowed her eyes at me. "What science lab?"

"You know that little lab," I replied impatiently. "The one on Denver Street. Just three streets from here."

"I don't hang out at weird little science labs," Anne said.

"Well, I don't either," I told her. "But I've passed by that lab a million times, riding my bike to school. I'm going to take this thing there. Someone will tell me what it is."

"I'm not going with you," Anne said, crossing her skinny arms in front of her chest. "I have better things to do."

"I didn't invite you," I sneered.

She sneered back at me.

I think she was jealous that I'd found the mysterious creature and she hadn't.

"Please get me the shoe box," I said. "I left it in your kitchen. I'm going to ride my bike over to that lab right now."

Anne went inside and came back with the shoe box. "It's all sticky inside," she said, making a disgusted face. "Whatever that thing is, it sure sweats a lot."

"Maybe your face scared it!" I declared. My turn to laugh. I'm usually the serious one. I don't make too many jokes. But that was a pretty good one.

Anne ignored it. She watched as I lowered the creature into the box. Then she raised her eyes to me. "You sure that isn't some kind of wind-up toy? This thing is all a big joke—isn't it, Dana?"

I shook my head. "No way. It's no joke. I'll stop by later and tell you what the scientists at the lab say about it."

I fitted the lid on the shoe box. Then I hurried to the garage to get my bike.

I couldn't wait to get to the science lab.

As it turned out, I should have stayed as far away from that place as possible.

But how could I know what was waiting for me there?

"Look out!"

Anne's stupid sheepdog ran in front of my bike just as I started down the driveway.

I jammed on the brakes. My bike squealed to a sharp stop—and the shoe box nearly toppled off the handlebars.

"Stubby—you moron!" I shrieked.

The dog loped off across the back garden, probably laughing to himself. I think Stubby gets a real thrill by tripping me up whenever he sees me.

I waited for my heart to stop thudding in my chest. Then I steadied the shoe box on the handlebars.

I started pedalling along the street, steering with one hand, keeping the other hand on top of the box.

"The scientists at the lab have got to know what this thing is," I told myself. "They've *got* to."

I usually speed down my street. But this morning I pedalled slowly. I stopped at each corner to make sure no cars were coming.

I tried to steer away from bumps in the street. But my street has a lot of potholes. Each time I hit a bump, I could hear the egg creature bouncing inside the box.

Just don't bounce out, I thought.

I pictured it bouncing out of the box, dropping on to the street, and being run over by a car.

I stopped to balance it better on the handle-bars. Then I began pedalling slowly again.

Some kids from school were starting up a soft-ball game on the playground on the next block. They called to me. I think they wanted me to join the game.

But I pretended I didn't hear them. I didn't have time for softball. I was on a scientific mission. I didn't look back. I kept pedalling.

As I turned the corner on to Denver Street, a city bus roared past. The whoosh of air from the bus nearly knocked me over.

As I steadied the bike, I saw the lid push up from the shoe box.

The egg creature was trying to escape!

I grabbed the box and tried to push down the lid. I pedalled faster. The lab was only a street away.

The creature pushed up against the lid.

I pushed back.

I didn't want to crush it. But I didn't want it to escape, either.

I could feel it bouncing inside the box. Pushing up against the lid.

I kept my hand on the lid, struggling to hold it down.

An estate car filled with kids rumbled past. One of the kids yelled something to me. I didn't really hear him. I was concentrating as hard as I could on keeping the egg creature inside the box.

I rolled through a stop sign. I didn't even see it. Luckily no cars were approaching.

The lab came into view on the next corner. It was a white shingled building. Very low. Only one storey tall. But very long. With a row of small, square windows along the front. It looked like a very long train carriage.

I bumped up the kerb and rode my bike on to the grass. Then I grabbed the shoe box with both hands and hopped off. The bike fell to the ground, both wheels spinning.

Gripping the box tightly in both hands, I ran across the front lawn, up to the white double doors in front.

I found a doorbell on the wall to the right of the doors. I pushed it. Pushed it again. Kept my finger on it.

When no one came to the door, I tried the knob. Pushed. Then pulled.

No. The door was locked.

I tried knocking. I pounded as hard as I could with my fist.

Then I rang the bell again.

Where was everyone?

I was about to start pounding again when I saw the sign over the door. A small, hand-printed black-and-white sign that sent my heart sinking. It read:

CLOSED SATURDAYS AND SUNDAYS.

I let out a long sigh and shoved the box under my arm. I was so disappointed. What was I going to do with this weird egg creature now?

Shaking my head unhappily, I turned and started back to my bike. I was halfway across the grass when I heard the front door open.

I turned to see an older man in a white lab coat. He had shiny white hair, parted in the middle and slicked down on the sides. His moustache was salt-and-pepper. He had pale blue eyes that peered out at me from his pale, wrinkly face.

His smile made his eyes crinkle up at the sides. "Can I help you?" he asked.

"Uh . . . yeah," I stammered. I raised the shoe box in front of me and started back across the grass. I could feel the egg creature bouncing around in there.

"Is that a sick bird?" the man asked, squinting

at the box. "I'm afraid I can't help you with that. This is a science lab. I'm not a vet."

"No. It's not a bird," I told him. I carried the box to the doorway. My heart was pounding. For some reason, I felt really nervous.

I guess I was excited about talking to a real scientist. I respect and admire scientists so much.

Also, I was excited about finally finding out what had hatched from that weird egg. And finding out what I should do with it.

The man smiled at me again. He had a warm, friendly smile that made me feel a little calmer. "Well, if it isn't a bird in there, what is it?" he asked softly.

"I was hoping you could tell me!" I replied. I shoved the shoe box towards him, but he didn't take it.

"It's something I found," I continued. "I mean, I found an egg. In my back garden."

"An egg? What kind of egg, son?"

"I don't know," I told him. "It was very big. And it had veins all over it. And it kind of breathed."

He stared at me. "An egg that breathed."

I nodded. "I put it in my dressing-table drawer. And then it hatched this morning. And—"

"Come in, son," the man said. "Come right in." His expression changed. His eyes flashed. He suddenly looked very interested.

He put a hand on my shoulder and guided me into the lab. I had to blink a few times and wait for my eyes to adjust to the dim light inside.

The walls were all white. I saw a desk and chairs. A low table with some science magazines on it. This was a waiting room, I decided. It was all very clean and modern-looking. A lot of chrome and glass and white leather.

The man had his eyes on the box in my hands. He rubbed his moustache with his fingers. "I'm Dr Gray," he announced. "I'm the managing lab scientist here."

I switched the box to my left hand so I could shake hands with him. "I want to be a scientist when I'm older," I blurted out. I could feel my face turning red.

"What's your name, son?" Dr Gray asked.

"Oh. Uh. Dana Johnson. I live a few blocks away. On Melrose Street."

"It's nice to meet you, Dana," Dr Gray said, straightening the front of his white lab coat. He moved to the front door. He closed it, locked it and bolted it.

That's weird, I thought, feeling a shiver of fear.

Why did he do that?

Then I remembered that the lab was closed on weekends. He probably bolts the doors when the place is closed.

"Follow me," Dr Gray said. He led the way

down the narrow white hallway. I followed him into a small lab. I saw a long table cluttered with all kinds of test tubes, specimen jars and electronic equipment.

"Set the box down there," he instructed, pointing to an empty spot on the table.

I set the box down. He reached in front of me to remove the lid. "You found this in your back garden?"

I nodded. "Back by the creek."

He carefully pulled the lid off the box.

"Oh my goodness!" he murmured.

The egg creature stared up at us. It quivered and bubbled against the side of the box. The bottom of the box was puddled with a sticky yellow goo.

"So you found one," Dr Gray murmured, tilting the box. The yellow blob slid to the other end.

"Found one?" I replied. "You mean you know what it is?"

"I thought I rounded them all up," Dr Gray replied, rubbing his moustache. He turned his pale blue eyes on me. "But I guess I missed one."

"What is it?" I demanded. "What kind of animal is it?"

He shrugged. He tilted the box the other way, making the egg creature slide to the other end. Then he gently poked the eggy blob in the back. "This is a young one," he said softly.

"A young *what*?" I asked impatiently.

"The eggs fell all over town," Dr Gray said,

302

poking the egg creature. "Like a meteor shower. Only on this town."

"Excuse me?" I cried. "They fell from the sky?" I wanted desperately to understand. But so far, nothing made sense.

Dr Gray turned to me and put a hand on my shoulder. "We believe the eggs fell all the way from Mars, Dana. There was a big storm on Mars. Two years ago. It set off something like a meteor shower. The storm sent these eggs hurtling through space."

My mouth dropped open. I gazed down at the quivering yellow blob in the shoe box. "This— this is a *Martian*?" I stammered.

Dr Gray smiled. "We think it came from Mars. We think the eggs flew through space for two years."

"But—but—" I sputtered. My heart was racing. My hands were suddenly ice cold.

Was I really staring at a creature from Mars?

Had I actually *touched* a Martian?

Then I had an even *weirder* thought: I found it. I picked it up from *my* back garden.

Did that mean it belonged to me?

Did I *own* a Martian?

Dr Gray bounced the creature—*my* creature—in the box. Its veins pulsed. Its black eyes stared back at us. "We don't know how the eggs made it through the earth's atmosphere," the scientist continued.

"You mean they should have burned up?" I asked.

He nodded. "Nearly everything burns up when it hits our atmosphere. But the eggs seem to be very tough. So tough they weren't destroyed."

The egg creature made a gurgling sound. It plopped wetly against the side of the shoe box.

Dr Gray chuckled. "This is a cute one."

"You have a lot of others?" I asked.

"Let me show you something, Dana." Holding the box in front of him, Dr Gray led the way through a large metal door. The door clanged heavily behind us.

A long, narrow hallway—the walls painted white—led past several small rooms. Dr Gray's lab coat made a starchy, scratchy sound as he walked. At the end of the hall, we stopped in front of a wide window.

"In there," Dr Gray said softly.

I stared into the window.

Then I stared harder.

Was he crazy? Was he playing some kind of joke on me?

"I—I can't see anything at all!" I cried.

304

"Hold on a second. I forgot something," Dr Gray said. He stepped over to the wall and flicked a light switch.

A light above our heads in the hallway flashed on. And now I could see through the window.

"Oh, wow!" I exclaimed as my eyes swept over the large room on the other side of the glass. I stared at a *crowd* of egg creatures!

Dozens of them.

Yellow, eggy blobs. All pulsing and quivering. Green veins throbbing.

The egg creatures huddled on the white tile floor. They looked like big globs of cookie dough on a baking sheet. Dozens of tiny, round black eyes stared out at us.

Unreal!

As I stared at them in amazement, I kept thinking they were like stuffed animals. But they weren't. They were alive. They breathed. They shook and bounced and bubbled.

305

"Would you like to go in?" Dr Gray asked.

He didn't wait for me to answer. He pulled out a small black control unit from his pocket. He pushed a button, and the door swung open. Then he opened the door wider and guided me inside.

"Whoa!" I uttered a cry when I felt a blast of cold air. "It's *freezing* in here!" I exclaimed.

Dr Gray smiled. "We keep it very cold. It seems to keep them more alert."

He held the shoe box in one hand. He motioned to the egg creatures with the other. "Once they hatch, the creatures don't like heat. If the temperature goes too high, they melt," he explained.

He lowered the box to the floor. "We don't want them to melt," he said. "If they melt, we can't study them."

Leaning over the box, he lifted my egg creature out gently. He placed it beside three or four other egg creatures. All of the yellow blobs began bouncing excitedly.

Dr Gray picked up the box and stood back up. He smiled down at the new arrival. "We don't want you to melt, do we?" he told it. "We want you to be nice and alert. So we keep it as cold in here as we can."

I shivered and rubbed my arms. I had goosebumps all over my skin. From the excitement? Or from the cold?

306

I wished I had worn something warmer than a T-shirt!

The egg creatures bobbed and bubbled. I couldn't take my eyes off them. Real creatures from Mars!

I watched them start to bounce towards us. They moved surprisingly fast. They kind of rolled, kind of inched their way forward. They left slimy, yellow trails behind them as they moved.

I wanted to ask Dr Gray a million questions. "Do they have brains?" I asked. "Are they smart? Can they communicate? Have you tried talking to them? Do they talk to each other? How can they breathe our air?"

He chuckled. "You have a good scientific mind, Dana," he said. "Let's take one question at a time. Which would you like me to answer first?"

'Well—" I started to reply. But I stopped when I realized what the egg creatures had done.

While Dr Gray and I talked, they had all moved quickly into a circle.

And now they had the two of us surrounded.

I spun around.

The egg creatures had moved behind us. They blocked the door. And now they were closing in on us, bubbling and throbbing, leaving a trail of slime as they slid forward.

What were they planning to do?

307

In a panic, I turned to Dr Gray. To my shock, he was grinning.

"They—they've trapped us!" I stammered.

He shook his head. "Sometimes they move like that. But don't be scared, Dana. They're harmless."

"Harmless?" I cried. My voice came out shrill and tiny. "But—but—"

"What can they do?" Dr Gray asked, placing a comforting hand on my trembling shoulder. "They're only blobs of egg. They can't bite you—can they? They don't appear to have mouths. They can't grab you. Or punch you. Or kick you. They have no hands or legs."

The egg creatures moved their circle closer. I watched them, my throat still tight, my legs shaking.

I knew that what Dr Gray was telling me was true.

But why were they doing this?

Why did they form a circle? Why were they closing in on us?

"Sometimes they form triangles," Dr Gray told me. "Sometimes rectangles or squares. It's as if they're trying out different shapes they've seen. Maybe this is a way they're trying to communicate with us."

"Maybe," I agreed softly. I wished the egg creatures would back away. They were little, wet blobs. But they were really giving me the creeps!

I shivered again. My breath steamed up in front of me.

It was so cold, my glasses started to fog!

I stared down at the egg creature I had brought. It had joined the circle. It bobbed and bounced with all the others.

Dr Gray turned and started to the door. I turned with him. I wanted to get out of that freezer as fast as I could!

"Thank you for bringing that one in," Dr Gray said. He shook his head. "I thought I had collected them all. What a surprise that I missed one." He scratched his hair. "You say you found it in your back garden?"

I nodded. "It was an egg. But then it hatched in my dressing-table drawer." My teeth chattered. I was so cold!

"Does that mean it's mine?" I asked Dr Gray. "I mean, does it belong to me?"

His smile faded. "I'm not really sure. I don't know what the law is about alien creatures from outer space." He frowned. "Maybe there *is* no law."

I glanced down at the little blob. The green veins along its side were bulging. Its whole body was throbbing like crazy.

Was it sorry to see me go?

No way. That's really dumb, I told myself.

"I guess you'll want to keep it for a while and study it," I said to Dr Gray.

He nodded. "Yes. I'm doing every kind of test I can think of."

"But can I come back and visit it?" I asked.

Dr Gray narrowed his eyes at me. "Come back? Dana, what do you mean by come back? You're not leaving."

17

"Excuse me?" I choked out. I knew I hadn't heard him correctly.

My whole body shook in a wild shiver. I rubbed my bare arms, trying to warm them.

"Did you say I'm not leaving?" I managed to ask.

Dr Gray locked his pale blue eyes on mine. "I'm afraid you can't leave, Dana. You must stay here."

A frightened cry escaped my throat. He wasn't serious! He couldn't be serious.

He can't keep me here, I told myself.

No way. He can't keep me here against my will. That's against the law.

"But ... why?" I demanded weakly. "Why can't I go home?"

"You can understand—can't you?" Dr Gray replied calmly. "We don't want anyone to know about these space aliens. We don't want anyone to know that we've been invaded by Martians."

He sighed. "You don't want to throw the whole world into a panic—do you, Dana?"

"I—I—I—" I tried to answer. But I was too frightened. Too startled. Too cold.

I glared angrily at Dr Gray. "You have to let me go," I insisted in a trembling whisper.

His expression softened. "Please don't stare at me like that," he said. "I'm not a bad guy. I don't want to frighten you. And I don't want to keep you in this lab against your will. But what choice do I have? I'm a scientist, Dana. I have to do my job."

I stared back at him, my whole body shaking. I didn't know what to say. My eyes moved to the metal door. It was shut. But he hadn't bolted it.

I wondered if I could get to the door before he did.

"I have to study *you* too," Dr Gray continued. He tucked his hands into the pockets of his lab coat. "It's my job, Dana."

"Study me?" I squeaked. "Why?"

He motioned to my egg creature. "You touched it—didn't you? You handled it? You picked it up?"

I shrugged. "Well, yeah. I picked it up. So what?"

"Well, we don't know what kind of dangerous germs it gave you," he replied. "We don't know what kind of germs or bacteria or strange diseases these things carried with them from Mars."

I swallowed hard. "Huh? Diseases?"

He scratched his moustache. "I don't want to scare you. You're probably perfectly okay. You feel okay—right?"

My teeth chattered. "Yeah. I guess. Just cold."

"Well, I have to keep you here and study you. You know. Watch you carefully. Make sure that touching the egg creature didn't harm you or change you."

No way, I thought.

I don't care about strange germs from Mars. I don't care about egg diseases. I don't care about science.

All I care about is getting out of here. Getting home to my family.

You're not keeping me here, Dr Gray. You're not studying me.

Because I'm *outta* here!

Dr Gray was saying something. I guess he was still explaining why he planned to keep me prisoner in this freezing cold lab.

But I didn't listen to him. Instead, I took off.

I ran towards the big metal door.

The circle of egg creatures blocked my way. But I leaped over them easily. And kept running.

Gasping for breath, shivering, I reached the door.

I grabbed the handle. And glanced back.

Was Dr Gray chasing after me?

No. He hadn't moved.

Good! I thought. I caught him by surprise.

I'm gone!

I turned the door handle. Pulled hard.

The door didn't open.

I pulled harder.

It didn't budge.

I tried pushing it.

No go.

Dr Gray's voice rang in my ears. "The door is controlled electronically," he said calmly. "It's locked. It cannot be opened unless you have the control unit."

I didn't believe him. I tugged again. Then I pushed again.

He was telling the truth. The door was electronically sealed.

I gave up with a loud cry of protest. I spun around to face him. "How long do I have to stay here?" I demanded.

He replied in a low, icy voice. "Probably for a very long time."

18

"Step away from the door, Dana," Dr Gray ordered. "Try to calm down."

Calm down?

"You'll be okay," the scientist said. "I take very good care of my specimens."

Specimens?

I didn't want to calm down. And I didn't want to be a specimen.

"I'm a boy. Not a specimen," I told him angrily.

I don't think he heard me. He lifted me out of the way. Then he clicked the small remote unit in his hand. The door opened just long enough for him to slide through.

It made a loud click as it snapped shut behind him.

Locked in. I was locked in this freezer with three dozen Martians.

My heart pounded. I heard a shrill whistle in my ears. My temples throbbed with pain. My whole head felt ready to explode!

315

I'd never been so angry in my life.

I let out a cry of rage.

The egg creatures all began to chatter, I spun around in surprise. They sounded a little like chimps.

A roomful of chimps, chattering away.

Only they weren't chimps. They were monsters from Mars. And I was locked in, all alone with them.

A specimen.

'Noooo!" I let out another howl and ran to the long window.

"You can't leave me here!" I shrieked. I pounded on the glass with both fists.

I wanted to cry. I wanted to scream until my throat was raw. I'd never felt so angry and so frightened all at once.

"Let me out! Dr Gray—let me out of here! You can't keep me here!" I screamed. I banged on the window as hard as I could.

I'll pound till I break the glass, I told myself.

I'll break through. Then I'll climb out and escape.

I beat my fists frantically against the glass. "Let me *out* of here! You can't *do* this!"

The glass was thick and hard. There was no way I could break through.

"*Let me out!*" I uttered a final scream.

When I turned back into the room, the egg

creatures stopped chattering. They stared up at me with their black, button eyes.

They didn't quiver or bounce. They stood totally still. As if they had frozen.

I'm going to freeze! I realized. I rubbed my bare arms. But it didn't help warm me. My hands were ice cold.

Icicles are going to form on me, I thought. I'm going to freeze to death in here. I'm going to turn into a human Popsicle.

The egg creatures stood so still. Their eyes were all locked on me. As if they were studying me. As if they were trying to decide what to do about me.

Suddenly my egg creature broke the silence. I recognized it by the blue veins down its front. It started to chatter loudly.

The other egg creatures turned, as if listening to it.

Was it talking to them? Was it communicating in some weird Martian chatter language?

"I hope you're telling them all how I saved your life!" I called to it. "I hope you're telling them what a good guy I am. You almost went down the drain—remember?"

Of course the egg creature couldn't understand me.

I don't know why I was shouting at it like that. I guess I was totally losing it. Totally freaked.

As the egg creature chattered on, I stared at

the others. They all listened in silence. I started to count them. There were so many of them—and so *few* of me!

Were they friendly? Did they like strangers? Did they like humans?

How did *they* feel about being locked up in this freezing cold room?

Did they feel anything at all?

These were questions I didn't really want to know the answers to.

I just wanted to get out of there.

I decided to try the window again. But before I could move, my egg creature stopped talking.

And the others started to move.

Silently, they huddled together. Pressed together into a wide yellow wedge.

And rolling faster than I could imagine, they attacked.

"Hey—!" I uttered a startled cry and backed up.

The wedge of egg creatures rolled forward. Their bodies slapped the floor wetly as they bounced towards me.

I retreated until my back hit the window.

Nowhere to run.

"What do you want?" I screamed. My voice came out high and tight in panic. "What are you going to do?"

I turned and banged on the window again, pounding with open hands. "Dr Gray! Dr Gray! Help me!"

Did they plan to roll over me? To swallow me up?

To my surprise, the egg creatures stopped a few inches in front of me. They twirled and bounced until they had formed a circle once again.

Then, moving quickly and silently, they shifted back into a big yellow triangle.

I stared down at them, shivering, my teeth chattering.

They're not attacking, I decided.

But what *are* they doing?

Why are they forming these shapes? Are they trying to *talk* to me?

I took a deep breath, trying to calm my panic.

You're a scientist, Dana, I reminded myself. Act like a scientist. Not a frightened kid. Try to talk back to them.

I thought hard for a few seconds. Then I raised my hands in front of me. And I formed a circle with my pointer fingers and thumbs.

I held the circle up so the egg creatures could all see it. And waited to see if they did anything.

The yellow blobs had formed a wide triangle that nearly filled the room. I saw their round black eyes go up to the circle I had formed.

And then I watched them bounce and roll—into a circle!

Were they copying me?

I straightened my fingers and thumbs into a triangle.

And the egg creatures formed a triangle.

Yes!

We're communicating! I realized. We're talking to each other!

I suddenly felt really excited. I felt like some kind of pioneer.

I'm the first person on earth to communicate with Martians! I told myself.

These creatures are friendly, I decided. They're not dangerous.

I didn't really know that for sure. But I was so excited that I had communicated with them, I didn't want to think anything bad about them.

Dr Gray has no right to keep them prisoner here, I thought.

And he has no right to lock me up with them.

I didn't believe his excuse for keeping me here. Not for a minute.

Just because I touched one? Just because I handled one?

Did he really expect me to believe that touching an egg creature could harm me?

Did he really think it would rot my skin off or something?

Did he really think that touching an egg creature would give me a weird disease or change me in some way?

That was just stupid.

I carried the little yellow blob in my hands — and I felt perfectly fine.

These creatures are my friends, I told myself. Touching them isn't going to harm me in any way.

But I'm a scientist. At least, I want to be a scientist. So I have to be scientific, I realized.

I decided to check myself out—just to make sure.

I raised my hands and inspected them carefully, first one, then the other. They looked okay to me. No strange rashes. No skin peeling off. I still had four fingers and a thumb on each hand.

I rubbed my arms. They were the same too. Perfectly okay.

Might as well check myself out all over, I told myself.

I reached down and grabbed my left leg.

Soft and mushy!

"Oh no!" I wailed.

I squeezed my leg again. Soft and lumpy.

I didn't have to look. I knew what was happening.

I was slowly turning into one of them. I was turning into a lump of scrambled eggs!

"No. Oh, please—no."

I squeezed my mushy ankle. I couldn't bear to look down. I didn't want to see what was happening to me.

But I had to.

Slowly, I lowered my gaze.

And saw that I was squeezing one of the egg creatures. Not my leg.

I let go instantly and raised my hand. A relieved laugh escaped my throat.

"Oh wow!"

How could I think that mushy blob was my leg?

I watched the little Martian scurry back to its pals.

I shook my head. Even though no one else was around, I felt like a total jerk.

Just calm down, Dana, I scolded myself.

But how could I?

The air in the lab seemed to get colder. I couldn't

stop shivering. I clamped my jaws tightly. But I couldn't stop my teeth from chattering.

I squeezed my nose. Cold and numb. I rubbed my ears. They were numb too.

This is no joke, I thought, my throat tightening. I'm going to get frostbite. I'm really going to freeze.

I tried thinking warm thoughts. I thought about the beach in summer. I thought about a blazing fire in the fireplace in our den.

It didn't help.

A hard shiver made my whole body twitch.

I've got to do something to take my mind off the cold, I decided.

The egg creatures had spread out over the room. I raised my hands again and formed a triangle.

They stared up at it, but didn't move.

I curled my fingers into a circle.

They ignored this one too.

"I guess you guys got bored, huh?" I asked them.

I tried to bend my fingers and thumbs into a rectangle. But it was too hard. Fingers and thumbs can't really bend into a rectangle.

Besides, the egg creatures weren't paying much attention to me.

I'm going to freeze, I told myself again. Freeze. Freeze. Freeze. The word repeated in my mind until it became an unhappy chant.

I lowered myself to the floor and pressed into the corner. I curled up, trying to save body warmth. Or what was left of it.

A sound on the other side of the window made me jump up.

Someone was coming. Dr Gray? To let me out?

I turned eagerly to the door. I heard footsteps out in the hall. Then a clink of metal.

A slot opened just above the floor to the left of the door. A food tray slid in. It plopped on to the floor.

I hurried over to it. Macaroni cheese and a small container of milk.

"But I *hate* macaroni cheese!" I screeched.

No reply.

"I hate it! I hate it! I hate it!" I wailed.

I was starting to lose it again. But I didn't care.

I leaned over the tray and held my hands over the plate of macaroni. The steam warmed my hands.

At least it's hot, I thought.

I sat down on the floor and lifted the tray to my lap. Then I gulped down the macaroni, just for the warmth.

It tasted horrible. I hate that wet, clotted, cheesy taste. But it did warm me up a little.

I didn't open the milk. Too cold.

Feeling a little better, I shoved the tray aside and climbed to my feet. I strode over to the window and started pounding the glass with my fists.

"Dr Gray—let me out!" I shouted. "Dr Gray—I know you can hear me. Let me out! You can't lock me in here and make me eat macaroni cheese! Let me out!"

I screamed until my voice was hoarse. I didn't hear a reply. Not a sound from the other side of the glass.

I turned away from the window in disgust.

"I've got to find a way out of here," I said out loud. "I've *got* to!"

And then, I had an idea.

Sad to say, it was a bad idea.

The kind of idea you think of when you're freezing to death in a total panic.

What was the idea? To call home and tell Mum and Dad to come and get me.

The only problem with that idea was that there were no phones in the room.

I searched carefully. There were metal shelves up to the ceiling against the back wall. They contained only scientific books and files. There was a desk in one corner. The desktop was bare.

Nothing else.

Nothing else in the whole room. Except for the dozens of egg creatures and me.

I needed another idea, an idea that didn't call for a telephone.

But I was stumped. I tried the door again. I thought Dr Gray might have been careless and left it unlocked.

No such luck.

I checked out the slot where my food tray had been delivered. It was only a few inches tall. Far too narrow for me to slip through.

I was trapped. A prisoner. A specimen.

I dropped glumly down to the floor and rested my back against the wall. I pulled up my knees and wrapped my arms around them. I curled into a ball, trying to stay warm.

How long did Dr Gray plan to keep me here? For ever?

I let out a miserable sigh. But then a thought helped to cheer me. I suddenly had a little hope.

I remembered something I had forgotten. I had told Anne where I was going!

This morning in her back garden, I had told Anne I was going to take the egg creature to the science lab.

I'm going to be rescued! I realized.

I leaped to my feet and shot both fists into the air. I opened my mouth in a happy cheer. "Yesssss!"

I knew exactly what would happen.

When I don't show up for dinner, Mum or Dad will call Anne. Because that's where I'm always hanging out when I should be home for dinner.

Anne will tell them I went to the science lab on Denver Street.

Mum will say, "He should be back by now."

Dad will say, "I'd better go get him."

And Dad will come and rescue me.

Only a matter of time, I knew. Only a matter of a few hours, and Dad will be here to get me out of this freezer.

I felt so much better.

I lowered myself back to the floor and leaned against the wall to wait. The egg creatures all stared at me. Watched me in silence. Trying to figure me out, I guess.

I didn't realize that I fell asleep. I guess I was worn out from all the excitement—and the fear.

I'm not sure how long I slept.

Voices woke me up. Voices from out in the hall.

I sat up, instantly alert. And I listened.

And heard Dad's voice.

Yes!

He was here. He was about to rescue me.

Yes!

I climbed to my feet. I stretched. I got ready to greet Dad.

And then, from the front hall, I heard Dr Gray say, "I'm sorry, Mr Johnson. Your son never stopped here."

"Are you sure?" I heard Dad ask.

"Very sure," Dr Gray replied. "I'm the only one here today. We're closed. We had no visitors."

"He's about this tall," I heard Dad say. "He has dark hair, and he wears glasses."

"No. Sorry," Dr Gray insisted.

"But he told his friend that he was coming here. He had something he wanted to show to a scientist. His bike is gone from the garage."

"Well, you can check outside for your son's bike," Dr Gray told Dad. "But I don't think you'll find it."

He moved it! I realized. Dr Gray moved my bike so no one would find it!

I let out a shout of rage and ran to the window. "Dad—I'm in here!" I shouted. I cupped my hands around my mouth so my voice would be even louder. "Dad! Can you hear me? I'm in here! Dad?"

I took a deep breath and listened. My heart

was thudding so loudly, I could hardly hear their voices from the front.

Dad and Dr Gray continued talking in low, calm voices.

"Dad! Can't you hear me?" I screamed. "It's me, Dana! Come back here, Dad! I'm here! Come and let me out!"

My voice cracked. My throat ached from screaming so loudly.

"Dad—*please!*"

My chest heaving, I pressed my ear against the window and listened again.

"Well, it's very strange, Mr Johnson," Dr Gray was saying. "The boy never came here. Would you like to look around the lab?"

Yes, Dad! I pleaded silently. *Say yes.*

Tell him that you'd like to look around the lab, Dad! Please!

"No thanks," I heard Dad say. "I'd better keep searching. Thank you, Dr Gray."

I heard Dad say goodbye.

I heard the front door close.

And I knew I was doomed.

"I don't believe this," I murmured out loud. "Dad was so close. So close!"

I sank back to the floor. I felt as if my heart were sinking too. I wanted to keep dropping, down on to the floor, into the ground. Just keep sinking till I disappeared for ever.

My throat ached from screaming. Why couldn't Dad hear me? I could hear him.

And why did he believe Dr Gray's lies? Why didn't Dad check out the lab for himself?

He would see me through the window. And I would be rescued.

Dr Gray is evil, I realized. He pretends to be interested only in science. He pretended to be worried about my health, about my safety. He said that's why he was keeping me here—to make sure I was safe.

But he lied to my father.

And he was lying to me.

332

Crouched on the floor, I shivered as the frigid air seemed to seep right through my skin. I shut my eyes and lowered my head.

I wanted to stay calm. I knew I had to stay calm to think clearly. But I couldn't. The chills I felt running down my back weren't just from the cold. They were also from terror.

Voices in the front snapped me to attention. I held my breath and listened.

Was that my dad?

Or was I starting to hear things?

"Maybe I *will* take a look around." That's what I thought I heard Dad say.

Was I dreaming it?

No. I heard Dr Gray mumble something. Then I heard Dad say, "Sometimes Dana sneaks into places where he doesn't belong. He's so interested in science, he may have sneaked in through a back door, Dr Gray."

"Yes!" I cried happily. Every time I lost all hope, I somehow got another chance.

I jumped up and hurried to the window. I crossed my fingers and prayed Dad would walk to the back and see me.

After a few seconds, I saw Dad and Dr Gray at the far end of the long, white hall. Dr Gray was leading him slowly, opening doors. They peered into each lab, then moved on.

"Dad!" I called. "Can you hear me? I'm back here!"

Even though I had my face pressed up to the window glass, he couldn't hear me.

I banged on the glass. Dad kept walking with Dr Gray. He didn't look up.

I waited for them to come closer. My heart was banging against my chest now. My mouth was dry. I pressed up close to the window.

In a few seconds, Dad would peer into the window and see me standing here.

And then I would be out—and Dr Gray would have some real explaining to do.

With my hands and nose pressed against the glass, I watched them move forward. The hall was dark at this end. But I could see them clearly as they peeked into the labs at the other end.

"Dad!" I shouted. "Dad—over here!"

I knew he couldn't hear me. But I had to shout anyway.

The two men disappeared into a lab for a few seconds. Then they came out and stepped towards me.

They were talking in low tones. I couldn't hear what they were saying.

Dad had his eyes on Dr Gray.

Turn this way, Dad, I silently urged. *Please— look to the end of the hall. Look in the window.*

Chatting softly, they disappeared through another door.

What on earth are they talking about? I wondered.

A few seconds later, they were back in the hall. Moving this way.

Dad—please! Here I am! I pressed up eagerly against the glass.

I pounded my fists on the window.

Dad looked up.

And stared into the window.

He stared right at me.

I'm rescued! I realized.

I'm outta here!

Dad stared at me for a few seconds.

Then he turned back to Dr Gray. "Thanks for showing me around," he said. "Dana definitely isn't here. Sorry I wasted your time."

"Dad—I'm right here!" I shrieked. "You're looking right at me!"

Was I invisible?

Why didn't he see me?

"Sorry I wasted your time, Dr Gray," I heard Dad say again.

"Good luck in finding Dana," Dr Gray replied. "I'm sure he'll turn up really soon. He's probably at a friend's house and forgot the time. You know how kids are."

"Nooooooo!" I let out a long wail. "Dad—come back! Dad!"

As I stared in horror, Dad turned away and started back down the long hall.

With another cry, I began to pound on the window glass with both fists. "Dad! Dad! Dad!" I chanted with each slam of my fist.

Dad turned around. "What's that noise?" he asked Dr Gray.

Dr Gray turned too.

I pounded the glass even harder. I pounded until my knuckles were raw and throbbing. "Dad! Dad! Dad!" I continued to chant.

"What's that pounding noise?" Dad demanded from halfway down the hall.

"It's the pipes," Dr Gray told him. "I've been having a lot of trouble with the pipes. The plumber is coming on Monday."

Dad nodded.

He kept walking. I heard him say goodbye to the scientist. Then I heard the door close behind him.

I knew that this time he wouldn't come back.

I didn't move from the window. I stared through the glass down the long hall.

A few seconds later, I saw Dr Gray coming towards me. He had an angry scowl on his face.

I'm his prisoner now, I thought glumly.

What does he plan to do?

He stopped outside the window. He clicked on the hall light.

In the bright light, I could see beads of sweat on his forehead. He frowned and stared in at me with those cold blue eyes.

"Nice try, Dana," he said sourly.

"Huh? What do you mean?" I choked out. My legs were trembling. Not from the cold. I was really terrified now.

"You almost got your father's attention," Dr Gray replied. "That wouldn't have been nice. That would have spoiled my plans."

I pressed both palms against the glass. I tried to force myself to stop trembling.

"Why couldn't Dad see me?" I demanded.

Dr Gray rubbed a hand over his side of the window. "It's one-way glass," he explained. "No one can see into the room from the hall—unless I turn on the bright hall light."

I let out a long sigh. "You mean—?"

"Your father saw only blackness," the scientist said with a pleased grin. "He thought he was staring into an empty room. Just the way you did—until I turned on the light."

"But why didn't he hear me?" I demanded. "I was shouting my head off."

Dr Gray shook his head. "A waste of time. The room you are in is totally soundproof. Not a sound escapes into the hall."

"But I can hear you!" I declared. "I could hear every word you and Dad said. And now you can hear me."

"There is a speaker system in the wall," he explained. "I can turn it on and off with the same control unit that locks the door."

"So I could hear you, but you couldn't hear me," I murmured.

"You're a very smart boy," he replied. His blue eyes flashed. "I know you're smart enough not to try any more tricks in there."

"You have to let me out!" I screamed. "You can't keep me here!"

"Yes, I can," he replied softly. "I can keep you here as long as I like, Dana."

"But—but—" I sputtered. I was so frightened, I couldn't speak.

"It's my duty to keep you in there," Dr Gray said calmly. He didn't care that I was so scared and upset. He didn't care about me at all, I realized.

He must be crazy, I decided.

Crazy and evil.

"It's my duty to keep you here," he repeated. "I must make sure that the egg creatures haven't harmed you. I must make sure that the egg creatures haven't given you strange germs that you might pass on to others."

"Let me out!" I shrieked. I was too frightened and angry to argue with him now. Too angry and frightened to think clearly. "Let me out! Let me out!" I demanded, pounding on the glass with my aching fists.

"Get some rest, Dana," he instructed. "Don't tire yourself out, son. I want to start doing tests on you in the morning. I have many, many tests to perform."

"But I'm f-freezing!" I stammered. "Let me out of here. At least let me stay somewhere warm. Please?"

He ignored my plea. He clicked off the hall light and turned away.

I watched him make his way down the long hall. He disappeared through a door in front. And closed the door hard behind him.

I stood there, trembling, my heart pounding.

I was cold—and very scared.

I had no way of knowing things were about to get a *lot* scarier!

I was so desperate to get Dad's attention, I nearly forgot about the egg creatures. Now I turned from the window to find them scattered around the room.

They stood still as statues. They didn't bounce or quiver. They all seemed to be staring at me.

Dr Gray had turned off the hall lights except for a tiny, dim bulb in the ceiling. The little egg blobs appeared pale and grey in the dim light.

I felt a chill at the back of my neck.

Was it safe to go to sleep in the same room with them?

I suddenly felt exhausted. So tired that all my muscles ached. My head spun.

I needed sleep.

I knew I had to rest so I could be alert and sharp tomorrow. Alert and sharp so I could find a way to escape.

But if I fell asleep, what would the egg creatures do?

Would they leave me alone? Would they sleep too?

Or would they try to harm me in some way?

Were they good? Were they evil?

Were they intelligent at all?

I had no way of knowing.

I only knew I couldn't stay awake much longer.

I dropped down to the floor and curled up in the corner. I tried to stay warm by tucking myself into a ball.

But it didn't help. The cold swept over me. My nose was frozen. My ears were numb. My glasses were frozen to my face.

Even wrapped up tightly, I couldn't stop shaking.

I'm going to freeze to death, I realized.

When Dr Gray comes back tomorrow morning, he'll find me on the floor. A solid lump of ice.

I gazed at the egg creatures. They stared back at me in the dim light.

Silence.

Such heavy silence in the room that I wanted to scream.

"Aren't you cold?" I cried out to them. My voice came out hoarse, weak from all the screaming I had done. "Aren't you freezing to death too?" I asked them. "How can you guys stand it?"

Of course they didn't reply.

"Dana, you're totally losing it," I scolded myself out loud.

I was trying to talk to a bunch of egg lumps from another planet! Did I really expect them to answer me?

They stared back in silence. None of them quivered. None of them moved. Their little dark eyes glowed in the dim light from the ceiling.

Maybe they're asleep, I thought.

Maybe they sleep with their eyes open. That's why they're not moving. That's why they've stopped bouncing. They're sound asleep.

That made me feel a little better.

I tucked myself into a tighter ball, and I tried to fall asleep too. If only I could stop shivering.

I closed my eyes and silently repeated the word, "sleep, sleep, sleep," in my mind.

It didn't help.

And when I opened my eyes, I saw the egg creatures start to move.

I was wrong. They weren't asleep.

They were wide awake. And they were all moving together. All moving at once.

Coming to get me.

"Ohhh." A low moan escaped from my throat.

I was already shaking all over from the cold. But now my entire body shuddered from fear.

The egg creatures moved with surprising speed.

They were bunching together in the centre of the room. Pressing into each other, making wet smacking sounds.

I tried to climb to my feet. But my legs didn't work.

My knees bent like rubber, and I landed back on the floor. I pressed back into the corner— and watched them move.

They slapped up against each other. Loud, wet slaps.

And as they pushed together, they rolled forward. Rolled towards me.

"What are you doing?" I cried in a high, shrill voice. "What are you going to do to me?"

They didn't reply.

The wet smacks echoed through the room as the egg creatures threw themselves into each other.

"Leave me alone!" I shrieked. Once again I tried to stand. I made it to my knees. But I was trembling too hard to balance on two feet.

"Leave me alone—please! I'll help you guys escape too!" I promised. "Really. I'll help you escape—tomorrow. Just let me make it through the night."

They didn't seem to understand.

They didn't seem to hear me!

What are they doing? I asked myself, watching them creep forward. Why are they doing this?

They had waited until I nearly fell asleep, I realized.

That means they wanted to catch me off guard. They wanted to sneak up on me.

Because they were about to do something I wasn't going to like. Something I wasn't going to like at all.

I pressed my back against the wall.

The egg creatures moved quickly now, pale in the grey light.

Squinting hard at them, I realized to my horror that they had all stuck themselves together.

They were no longer dozens of little egg creatures.

Now they had joined together to form *one enormous egg creature*!

I was staring at a big, quivering *wall* of egg! A wall so big it nearly covered the floor of the room.

A wall that was rolling towards me. Rolling to get me.

"Whoa! Please—whoa!" I choked out.

I knew I should climb to my feet. I knew I should try to run.

But where could I run?

How could I escape from this huge, solid egg wall?

I couldn't.

So I lay there and watched it come. Too frozen. Too frozen to move.

"Ohhhh." I moaned as the front of the wall of eggs rose up over my shoes.

It was moving so fast now. Crawling somehow.

Crawling over me.

The egg wall swept over my shoes. Over the legs of my jeans. Over my waist.

I lay there helpless as it swept over me.

Too frozen. Too frozen.

Helpless, as it poured over me.

Trapping me beneath it.

Smothering me.

I should have moved.

I should have fought it.

Too late. Too late now.

The sticky, warm egg creatures—all glued together—rolled over me like a heavy carpet.

I pushed up both arms. I raised my knees. I tried to squirm away.

Too late.

I tried to roll out from underneath. But the heavy, living carpet had me pinned on my back. Pinned to the floor.

It rolled over my waist. And then quickly, over my chest.

Was it going to sweep over my head? Was it going to smother me?

I punched at it with both fists.

But it was too late to push it away. Too late to do it any harm.

Too late to stop it as it crept closer to my neck. So warm and heavy.

I twisted my head from side to side. I tried to roll away.

But it was no use.

Too late. Too late to fight back.

And now I lay there, trapped. And felt it creep up to my chin.

Felt it throbbing. Pulsing.

Dozens of eggy monsters all pressed together. Alive. A living sheet of egg creatures. Covering me.

Covering me.

I took a deep breath and held it as the heavy, warm carpet pressed itself against my chin. My arms and legs were pinned to the floor. I couldn't squirm away.

I couldn't move.

To my surprise, the egg carpet stopped under my chin.

I let out a long whoosh of air.

And waited.

Had it really stopped?

Yes.

It didn't crawl over my head. It rested heavily on top of me. Throbbing steadily, as if it had two dozen heartbeats.

So warm.

I felt so warm beneath it. Almost cosy.

I let out a sigh. For the first time, I had stopped shivering. My hands and feet were no longer frozen. No chills ran down my back.

Warm. I felt toasty and warm.

A smile spread over my face. I could feel my fear fading away with the cold.

The egg creatures weren't trying to harm me, I realized.

They wanted to help me.

They pressed themselves together to form a blanket. A warm and cosy blanket.

They worked together to keep me from freezing.

They saved my life!

With the warm, pulsing blanket on top of me, I suddenly felt calm. And sleepy. I drifted into a peaceful, dreamless sleep.

Such a wonderful, soothing sleep.

But it didn't help get me ready for the horrors of the next morning.

I awoke a couple of times during the night. At first, I felt alarmed and frightened when I saw that I wasn't home in bed.

But the pulsing, warm egg blanket relaxed me. I shut my eyes and drifted back to sleep.

Some time in the morning, I was aroused from a deep sleep by an angry voice. I felt hands grab my shoulders roughly.

Someone was shaking me hard. Shaking me awake.

I opened my eyes to find Dr Gray bending over me in his white lab coat. His face was twisted in anger. He shook me hard, shouting furiously.

"Dana—what have you done? What have you done to the egg monsters?"

"Huh?" I was still half asleep. My eyes struggled to focus. My head bobbed loosely on my shoulders as the angry scientist shook me.

"Let me go!" I finally managed to choke out.

"What have you done to them?" Dr Gray

350

demanded. "How did you turn them into a blanket?"

"I—I didn't!" I stammered.

He uttered a furious growl. "You've ruined everything!" he shrieked.

"Please—" I started, struggling to wake up.

He let go of me and grabbed the egg blanket in both hands. "What have you done, Dana?" he repeated. "Why did you do this?"

With another cry of rage, he ripped the blanket off me—and heaved it against the wall.

The egg creatures made a soft *splat* as they hit the lab wall. I heard them utter tiny squeals of pain. The blanket folded limply to the floor.

"You shouldn't do that, Dr Gray!" I screamed, finally finding my voice. I jumped to my feet. I could still feel the warmth of the egg blanket on my skin.

"You hurt them!" I shrieked.

I gazed down at the yellow blanket. It bubbled silently where it had been thrown. It didn't move.

"You let them touch you?" Dr Gray demanded, twisting his face in disgust. "You let them cover you up?"

"They saved my life!" I declared. "They pushed together to make a warm blanket—and they saved my life!"

I glanced down again. The egg creatures remained stuck together. The blanket appeared

351

to be seething now. Throbbing hard. As if excited. Or angry.

"Are you crazy?" Dr Gray cried, his face red with anger. "Are you crazy? You let these *monsters* rest on top of you? You touched them? You handled them? Are you trying to destroy my discovery? Are you trying to destroy my work?"

He's the crazy one, I realized. Dr Gray isn't making any sense. He isn't making any sense at all.

He moved quickly—and grabbed me again. Held me in a tight grip so I couldn't escape. And pulled me to the door.

"Let go of me! Where are you taking me?" I demanded.

"I thought you could be trusted," Dr Gray replied in a menacing growl. "But I was wrong. I'm so sorry, Dana. So sorry. I had hoped to keep you alive. But I see now that is impossible."

He dragged me to the door. He stopped and reached into the pocket of his lab coat. Reached for the control unit to open the door.

I saw my chance. He had me by only one hand. With a hard burst of strength, I pulled away. He let out a cry. Reached both hands for me. Missed.

I ran to the other side of the lab. I turned at the wall to face him.

He had a strange smile on his face. "Dana, there's nowhere to run," he said softly.

My eyes flashed around the room. I don't know what I was searching for. I had seen it all. And I knew that he was telling the truth.

Dr Gray stood blocking the only door. The long window was too heavy and thick to break through. And it didn't open.

There were no other windows. No other doors. No ways to escape.

"What are you going to do now, Dana?" Dr

Gray asked softly, the strange smile stuck on his face. His blue eyes locked coldly on mine. "Where are you going to go?"

I opened my mouth to reply. But I had nothing to say.

"I'll tell you what's going to happen," Dr Gray said softly, calmly. "You're going to stay in here. In this cold, cold room. I'm going to leave you now and make sure you're locked in."

His smile grew wider. "Then do you know what I'm going to do? Do you?"

"What?" I choked out.

"I'm going to make it colder in here. I'm going to make it colder than a freezer."

"No—!" I protested.

His smile faded. "I trusted you, Dana. I trusted you. But you broke that trust. You let them touch you. You let them form this—this carpet! You ruined them, Dana! You ruined my egg monsters!"

"I—I didn't do anything!" I stammered. I squeezed my hands into fists. But I felt so helpless. Helpless and afraid.

"You can't freeze me in here!" I cried. "I didn't do anything! You can't leave me in here to freeze!"

"Of course I can," Dr Gray replied coldly. "This is my lab. My own little world. I can do whatever I want."

He pulled the little black remote unit from his

lab coat pocket. He pointed it at the door and pushed a button.

The door swung open.

He started to leave. "Goodbye, Dana," he called.

"No—stop!" I called.

Dr Gray turned from the doorway.

And as he turned, the blanket of egg creatures rose up.

It stood straight up—and flung itself over him. It dropped on top of the scientist with a hard *thud*.

"Hey—" He let out an angry cry. The cry was muffled by the heavy yellow blanket of egg creatures.

The egg blanket covered him. I watched him struggle underneath it. And I listened to his muffled cries.

He was squirming and twisting beneath the blanket. But he couldn't toss it off. And he couldn't slide out from under it.

He crumpled to the floor, and the blanket crumpled with him.

I watched it seething and bubbling on top of him.

Then I didn't wait another second. I took a deep breath—and I ran across the room. I darted past the egg blanket with Dr Gray twisting and thrashing underneath it.

I ran out of the door.

Down the long hall to the front of the lab.

Yes! A few seconds later, I pushed open the front door and burst outside. Breathing hard, sucking in the sweet, fresh air.

A beautiful morning. A red ball of a sun still rising over the spring-green trees. The sky clear and blue.

I glanced around. I could see a paper-boy on his bike halfway up the block. No one else on the street.

I turned and ran around to the side of the building. The grass smelled so wonderful! The morning air so warm and fresh. I was so thrilled to be outside!

I had to get home.

I had a hunch—and the hunch was right. I spotted my bike, resting against the back wall of the lab, hidden by a large rubbish bin.

I leapt on to it and started to pedal. Riding a bike never felt as exciting, so *thrilling*!

I was getting away, away from the horror of crazy Dr Gray and his freezing lab.

I pedalled faster. I rode without stopping. Without *seeing*! The world was a blur of green.

I must have set a speed record for getting

home. I roared up the driveway, the tyres sending gravel flying on both sides.

Then I jumped off my bike and let it topple to the grass. I dived for the kitchen door and burst into the kitchen. "Mum!" I cried.

She jumped up from the breakfast table. I caught the worried expression on her face. It melted away as I ran into the room.

"Dana!" she cried. "Where *were* you? We've all been so terrified. The police are looking for you and—and—"

"I'm okay!" I told her. I gave her a quick hug.

Dad ran in from the hallway. "Dana—you're okay? Where *were* you all night? Your mother and I—"

"Egg monsters!" I cried. "Egg monsters from Mars! Hurry!" I grabbed Dad's hand and tugged. "Come on!"

"Huh?" Dad spun around. He narrowed his eyes, studying me. "What did you say?"

"No time to explain!" I gasped. "They've got Dr Gray. He's evil, Dad. He's so evil!"

"Who has *what*?" Mum demanded.

"The egg creatures! From Mars! Hurry! There's no time!"

They didn't move. I saw them exchange glances.

Mum stepped forward and placed a hand on my forehead. "Do you have a fever, Dana? Are you sick?"

358

"No!" I screamed. "Listen to me! Egg creatures from Mars! Follow me!"

I know I wasn't explaining myself too well. But I was frantic.

"Dana—come and lie down," Mum instructed. "I'll call Dr Martin."

"No—please! I don't need a doctor!" I protested. "Just follow me—okay? You've got to see them. You've got to see the egg creatures. You've got to hurry."

Mum and Dad exchanged worried glances again.

"I'm not crazy!" I shrieked. "I want you to come with me to the science lab!"

"Okay, okay," Dad finally agreed. "You were in that lab last night?"

"Yes," I told him, shoving him to the kitchen door. "I called and called. But you couldn't hear me."

"Oh, wow," Dad murmured, shaking his head. "Wow."

The three of us climbed into the car.

It took about three minutes to drive to the lab. Dad parked in front. I jumped out of the car before he stopped.

The front door to the lab stood wide open, as I'd left it.

I ran inside with Mum and Dad close behind me.

"They're egg creatures," I told them breathlessly. "They dropped down from Mars. They captured Dr Gray."

I led the way down the long hall.

I pushed open the door to the freezing back room.

Mum and Dad stepped in behind me.

I gazed around the room—and gasped in amazement!

I saw Mum and Dad staring at me. They had worried expressions on their faces.

"Where are the egg creatures?" Mum demanded softly.

Dad rested a hand gently on my shoulder. "Where are they, Dana?" he asked in a whisper.

"Uh . . . they're gone," I choked out.

The lab stood empty.

No Dr Gray. No egg creatures. No one.

Bare white walls. Nothing on the floor.

Nothing.

"Maybe they went back to Mars," I murmured, shaking my head.

"And Dr Gray? What about Dr Gray?" Dad asked.

"Maybe they took Dr Gray with them," I replied.

"Let's go home," Mum sighed. "Let's get you into bed, Dana."

Dad guided me from the room, his hands on

my shoulders. "I'll call Dr Martin," he said softly. "I'm sure we can get him to come to the house this morning."

"I—I do feel a little strange," I admitted.

So they drove me home and tucked me into bed.

The doctor came later that morning and examined me. He didn't find anything wrong. But he said I should stay in bed and rest for a while.

I knew that Mum and Dad didn't believe my story. I felt bad about that. But I didn't know how to convince them I was telling the truth.

I did feel a little weird.

Just tired, I guess.

I dozed off and woke up and dozed off again.

In the afternoon, I woke up to hear my sister Brandy talking to some friends outside my room. "Dana totally freaked out," I heard Brandy say. "He says he was kidnapped by egg monsters from Mars."

I heard Brandy's friends giggling.

Oh great, I thought bitterly. Now everyone thinks I'm a nut case.

I wanted to call Brandy into my room and tell her what really happened. I wanted to make her believe me. I wanted to make *someone* believe me.

But how?

I fell asleep again.

I was awakened by a voice calling my name. I sat up in bed. The voice floated in from my open bedroom window.

I climbed out of bed and made my way to the window. Anne was calling me from the driveway. "Dana—are you okay? Do you want to come over? I've got a new CD-ROM version of *Battle Chess.*"

"Cool!" I called down to Anne. "I'll be right over."

I pulled on a T-shirt and a pair of jeans. I was feeling pretty good. Rested. Like my old self.

So happy that everything was back to normal.

I hummed to myself as I brushed my hair. I stared at myself in the mirror.

You had an amazing adventure, Dana, I told myself. Imagine—you spent the night with egg creatures from Mars!

But now you're okay, and your life is back to normal.

I felt so happy, I gave Brandy a hug on my way down the stairs. She stared at me as if I truly were crazy!

Humming loudly, I made my way out the kitchen door and started across the garden to Anne's house.

Everything looked so beautiful to me. The grass. The trees. The spring flowers. The sun setting behind the trees.

What a day! What a beautiful, perfect, normal day!

And then halfway across Anne's lawn, I stopped.

I crouched down on the grass—and I laid the biggest egg you ever saw!

Goosebumps

R.L.Stine

Reader beware, you're in for a scare!

These terrifying tales will send shivers up your spine:

Goosebumps

Give Yourself Goosebumps

A scary new series from R.L. Stine – where *you* decide what happens!

Choose from over 20 scary endings!

GOOSEBUMPS

Reader beware – here's THREE TIMES the scare!

Look out for these bumper GOOSEBUMPS editions. With three spine-tingling stories by R.L. Stine in each book, get ready for three times the thrill … three times the scare … three times the GOOSEBUMPS!

HIPPO GHOST

Secrets from the past... Danger in the present...
Hippo Ghost brings you the spookiest of tales...

Castle of Ghosts
Carol Barton
Abbie's *bound* to see some ghosts at the castle where
her aunt works – isn't she?

The Face on the Wall
Carol Barton
Jeremy knows he must solve the mystery of the face on
the wall – however much it frightens him...

Summer Visitors
Carol Barton
Emma thinks she's in for a really boring summer, until she
meets the Carstairs family on the beach. But there's
something very *strange* about her new friends...

Ghostly Music
Richard Brown
Beth loves her piano lessons. So why have they started to
make her *ill*...?

A Patchwork of Ghosts
Angela Bull
Who is the evil-looking ghost tormenting Lizzie, and why
does he want to hurt her...?

The Ghosts who Waited
Dennis Hamley
Everything's changed since Rosy and her family moved
house. Why has everyone suddenly turned against her...?

The Railway Phantoms
Dennis Hamley
Rachel has visions. She dreams of two children in strange,
disintegrating clothes. And it seems as if they are trying
to contact her. . .

The Haunting of Gull Cottage
Tessa Krailing
Unless Kezzie and James can find what really happened in
Gull Cottage that terrible night many years ago, the
haunting may never stop. . .

The Hidden Tomb
Jenny Oldfield
Can Kate unlock the mystery of the curse on Middleton
Hall, before it destroys the Mason family. . . ?

The House at the End of Ferry Road
Martin Oliver
The house at the end of Ferry Road has just been built.
So it can't be haunted, can it. . . ?

Beware! This House is Haunted
This House is Haunted Too!
Lance Salway
Jessica doesn't believe in ghosts. So who *is* writing the
strange, spooky messages?

The Children Next Door
Jean Ure
Laura longs to make friends with the children next door.
But they're not quite what they seem. . .

The Girl in the Blue Tunic
Jean Ure
Who is the strange girl Hannah meets at school – and
why does she seem so alone?